MILLENIUM
PROJECT PENDULUM

Suddenly Eric felt with full force the impact of his twin brother's absence. The strangeness, the aloneless, the separateness.

It came rushing in like a roaring tidal wave: the knowledge that time stood between him and his brother like a sword. At this very moment Sean was a hundred miles away, back at the minus-fifty-minute level. The balancing swing of the pendulum, the equal and opposite displacement.

From here to Time Ultimate — the end of the experiment, some ninety-five million years out from the starting point — they were never going to be on the same side of the time-line again.

Other books in the Millenium science-fiction/fantasy series include:

PROJECT PENDULUM

Robert Silverburg

BEAVER BOOKS

A Beaver Book

Published by Arrow Books Limited
20 Vauxhall Bridge Road, London SW1V 2SA

An imprint of Random Century Group

London Melbourne Sydney Auckland
Johannesburg and agencies throughout
the world

First pub shed in Great Britain in 1989 by
H chinson Children's Books
Beaver edition 1990

*Millenium Books and the Millenium symbol are trademarks of
Byron Preiss Visual Publications, Inc.*

Book edited by David M. Harris

*Special thanks to Kirby McCauley, Jean-Marc Officier and
Elisabeth Wansborough*

Printed and bound in Great Britain by
Courier International Ltd, Tiptree, Essex

ISBN 0 09 962460 5

For Jim and Greg Benford

Displacement hit him like a punch in the gut. He had to fight to keep from doubling up, coughing and puking. He was dizzy, too, and his legs kept trying to float up towards the ceiling. But the sensation lasted only a fraction of a second, and then he felt fine.

He was still in the laboratory, standing right in front of himself. In front of Sean, too. Twin and twin. Sean and the other version of himself were sitting side by side on the shunt platform in their strange little three-legged metal chairs, waiting for it all to begin.

Five minutes from now the singularity coupling would come to life and the displacement force would take hold of them. And they would be shuttled at infinite speed between the black hole and the white hole until they were thrust out through the time gate. But right now they were staring in wonder and amazement at him – at the extra Eric, $Eric_2$, the one who had been conjured up out of the mysterious well of time. Who had been pulled five minutes out of the future to stand before them now.

Weird to be looking at yourself like this, Eric thought. Seeing yourself from the outside.

In a sense, of course, he had had a way of seeing himself from the outside all his life. He just needed to glance at his twin brother, Sean. Looking at Sean's eyes was almost like looking into a mirror. The same colour, the same glinting alertness. The same quick motions, taking everything in.

But this was different. Sean was like a mirror image of him, and your mirror image is never what you are. Eric didn't feel he looked as much like Sean as everyone else seemed to think, anyway. But now he was looking at *himself*, not Sean. Seeing neither his twin brother nor his own mirror image, but seeing himself unreflected, as others saw him all the time.

Strange. His nose – the nose of the other Eric – didn't seem right and his smile turned the wrong way at the corners of his mouth. His eyebrows were reversed, with the one on the right side pointing up. His whole face looked out of balance.

Eric wandered around the lab like some sort of disembodied spirit, prowling here and there. Someone aimed a camera at him and he made faces into it, putting his hands to his ears and wiggling them.

Dr Ludwig said, 'Five minutes exactly. Perfect displacement. Perfect visibility.'

'Paradox number one,' Dr White chimed in. 'The duplication. The overlap of identity.'

'And paradox number two, also. The cumulative and self-modifying aspects of the time-stream correction.'

'Say that again?' Eric asked.

Ludwig didn't trouble to reply. He glowered and scowled and vanished into the flow of his own intricate thoughts. It seemed to bother him that Eric had spoken at all. As if Eric were nothing more than an irritating

8

distraction at this very complicated moment.

All around the room, technicians were throwing switches and tapping commands into terminals. Everybody was tense. To all these people Time Zero, the moment of the initial shunt, was still four and a half minutes away. The final delicate calibrations and balances had to be made.

Some of the staff people were staring at him the way they might stare at a ghost. That puzzled him for a moment. They should be used to backward-going time travellers by now. After all, Sean had already come this way on the minus-fifty-minute shunt, hadn't he? And Eric would be doing the minus-five-hundred-minute one himself a few hours ago. Even though he hadn't experienced it yet, *they* had. Or should have.

But then Eric recalled what they had told him about these past-changing paradoxes. Each swing of the pendulum retroactively corrected everybody's memories and perceptions. That was how it had been in the earlier experiments with robots and animals and they expected it to work the same this time. Nobody remembered Sean's minus-fifty-minutes appearance, or any of the earlier ones, because they hadn't happened yet. But as the pendulum kept swinging, those appearances *would* happen, at times earlier than this, and the corrections would be made, and everyone would begin to remember a past that right now didn't yet exist. Or something like that. It made no sense if you tried to think of it in the old straight-line way. Now that time travel was a fact, no one could think that way ever again.

Warning lights were lit up on all the instrument panels now. Critical displacement momentum was nearly attained. Sean and that other Eric would be on their way in another few instants. And he'd be moving along, too. He couldn't stay here much longer. Any minute now the next $Eric_2$ would be making the journey from Time Zero back to minus-five-minutes, the journey that he himself had just taken. The mathematics of time wouldn't allow him still to be here when the loop began all over again. You could have an Eric and an $Eric_2$ in the same place at the same time, but not more than one $Eric_2$. He would have to be up and out, swinging towards his second stop, the plus-fifty-minute level.

He could feel the force pulling at him now.

Eric waved jauntily at the Eric and Sean on the platform. When shall we three meet again? he asked himself. Probably never. He'd see Sean again at the end of the experiment, sure. If all went well. But there was no reason why he should ever come face to face with himself a second time.

Which was just as well, he decided. There's something creepy about looking yourself in the eye.

'Have a good trip, guys!' he called out to them. And the force seized him and swept him away into the time-stream.

2

Sean + 5 minutes

And then at long last they threw the final switch, the one that would send him spinning off into the vast distant reaches of time, and nothing happened. At least that was how it felt to Sean at first. No blinding flashes of light, no strangely glowing haloes, no sinister humming sounds, no sense of turbulent upheaval. Nothing. An odd calmness, even a numbness, seemed to envelop him. So far as he could tell, nothing had changed at all. He was still sitting right where he had been, on the left-hand focal point of the singularity coupling.

Maybe it was too soon. Only an instant had passed, after all. Maybe the displacement cone was still building up energy, still gathering the momentum it would need to hurl him across the centuries.

A moment later Sean started finding out how wrong he was.

That first moment of calm began to fade as bits of data came flooding into his mind: scattered and trivial bits at first, adding up very quickly into something overwhelming. Subtle wrongnesses became apparent, little ones that quickly grew bigger and bigger in his mind:

 –Dr Ludwig, who had been over by Eric's side of the singularity coupling when the last switch was thrown, had moved to his left, barely outside the event horizon of the shunt field.

– Dr White, who had been all the way across the big room in front of the bank of monitor screens frantically fidgeting with her thick curling hair, was now leaning calmly against the frame of the lab door with her arms folded.

– The computer printers, which had been standing silent in the moment before the throwing of the switch, were spewing copy like crazy. The frontmost one had an inch-thick stack of pages in its hopper.

– Half a dozen technicians who had been scattered here and there around the room were gathered in a tight cluster just beyond the gleaming nickel-jacketed hood of the field shield. They were staring at Sean as though he had sprouted a second head – or had lost the one he used to have.

– And more. The pattern of lights on the instrument panels was different. Someone had restrung the tangle of drooping grey cables on the back wall. And the video camera dolly had been pushed about halfway down the track in his direction. It had been in front of Eric before. At least a dozen tiny changes of that sort had been made.

It was, he thought, very much like one of those before-and-after blackout tests they give you when you're a kid, when they want to measure your IQ. They show you the image of a room, and then the screen goes dark, and a moment later it lights up and everything's been moved around. You have to note down as many of the changes as you can pick out, within thirty seconds or so. That was what had happened here. In the twinkling of an eye, *before* had turned into *after*. Five minutes after.

So he really had taken a leap through time.

After all the months and months of planning and training and doubting and hoping, he had finally embarked on this fantastic voyage into the remote past and the far-off unknown future, a voyage that would unfold in a series of jumps. Small jumps at first, and then unimaginably vast.

Jump number one. He was five minutes in his own future. All the little changes around the room told him that.

And now he noticed the biggest change of all, the one he had somehow managed to keep blocked from his awareness until this moment – Eric wasn't there any more.

Eric's three-legged aluminium chair was still there, to the right of the singularity coupling. But Eric himself was gone.

Sean felt dazed. A thick oily fog was trying to wrap itself around his brain. It was like a delayed reaction coming on, the whole crushing weight of the knowledge that he had actually been ripped out of space and time and then had been thrust back into place somewhere else.

'How do you feel, Sean?' Dr Ludwig asked. The words were like rolling thunder in Sean's ears. He had to work hard to wring some sense from the blurred, blooming sounds.

'Not bad,' he said automatically. 'Not bad at all.'

He kept staring at the empty chair to his right, beyond the cone of the displacement torus. Eric wasn't there. Eric wasn't there. That was the only thought in his mind. Suddenly it had driven even the fact of the time voyage itself from the centre of his consciousness.

For the entire twenty-three years of Sean's life, Eric had always been there. Somewhere. Maybe not close at hand

13

but always in some way *there*. They could be on opposite sides of the continent and yet they always remained aware of each other's presence in some mysterious, indefinable way that neither of them tried to understand or explain. It had been like that for them all the way back to the beginning, to that time when they had shared the same womb, Eric lying beside him, jostling for space, poking his little arms and legs where they didn't belong.

Sean had never been alone like this before.

He had understood that the experiment was going to separate them in time, sending Eric one way, him another. But there is understanding and there is understanding. There are things you understand in your mind, and there are things you understand in your bones. Now that the contact between them had actually been severed, he was coming fully to realize what it meant to be separated from his twin by an enormous and uncrossable gulf of time. That was different. That was terrifying.

'Sean?' Dr Ludwig said again, rumbling and strange as before. 'I asked you how you were feeling.'

'Not bad, I told you.' He turned, stared, worked hard at focusing his eyes. He was getting some odd visual effects now. Streaks of coloured lights, reds and blues and greens. Everything seemed too long and narrow. And there was some double vision. He was dimly aware that Dr Ludwig was still talking to him. And Dr White, too. Their words came to him from a million miles away. How are you feeling, how are you feeling, how are you feeling. What did that mean? Oh. It means how are you feeling, he thought. Is that any of their business? He was so terribly confused.

'Sean—'

'I'm all right!' he snapped. He didn't want them to think he couldn't take it.

They looked at him blankly. He tried to explain things,

14

but he had the feeling his words were ricocheting around them like bullets. They turned to each other in bewilderment.

'What did he say?'

'Sean? Try to speak more slowly. You're all hyped up.'

'Am I? You sound all slowed down.'

It was getting worse. He felt that his own chair was melting and flowing beneath him. And he was starting to melt with it. A sense of chill and a sense of burning at the same time. A strangeness in his stomach. A rising and a falling in his chest. That first calm moment when nothing seemed to have changed seemed like a million years ago. Everything was changing now. Everything. He wondered if Eric was feeling anything like this. Wherever Eric was right now. *When*ever Eric was.

'Maybe my voice will be easier for you to make out, Sean.'

That was Dr White. Speaking gently, softly, carefully. Her voice sounded deeper than it should have been, but not as strange as Dr Ludwig's.

Sean tried to force himself to relax. He said, making an effort to be understood, 'What was the span of the jump, Dr White?'

'Five minutes precisely. Right on target.'

'And how long has it been since I got here?'

'Fifteen, twenty seconds.'

That was all? It felt like half an hour. His mind was feeding him distorted information. Was this how it was going to be, on and on through time, everything blurred and confused? Like a nightmare? Stumbling across millions of years in a dopey fog, understanding nothing?

'What have you heard from my brother?' Sean asked.

'Your brother's fine.' Dr Ludwig's voice.

'You've heard from him?'

'We saw him. Five minutes before Time Zero.'

15

Sean frowned and shook his head. Everything was so hard to follow.

'Five minutes before the shunt? Well, yes, but what I meant was . . .' He paused. He didn't know what he meant. 'I know you saw my brother then. You saw both of us then, right here. But—'

'We saw him and we saw you.' The soft voice of Dr White. 'But we saw an extra Eric also, $Eric_2$, the one travelling backwards from Time Zero. Don't you remember that?'

'An extra Eric.' He felt so *stupid*.

'Smiling at us. Winking. Happy and confident.'

'Travelling backwards,' Sean murmured, struggling to cut through the fog in his brain. 'An extra Eric.'

So muddled, his mind. His fine mind, his outstanding mind. He wondered if he'd ever be able to do physics again. Or even simply to think straight. He shook his head again, slowly, heavily, like a wounded bear.

They had seen Ricky travelling backwards in time. Saw him arrive five minutes before Time Zero, before the start of the experiment. In this very room. Why can't I remember seeing him? Or do I? I think I do, yes. Sean closed his eyes a moment. He tried to imagine the scene.

That ghostly figure, hovering in front of them, looking so very cheerful. Ricky always looked cheerful, even at crazy times. So there had been one Eric Gabrielson sitting in the right-hand chair on the shunt platform and another one, $Eric_2$, floating around the middle of the room. And that had been five minutes before Time Zero – the shunt that balanced this one that had carried him five minutes beyond Time Zero. The first swing of the giant pendulum that would cut across millions of years, carrying them backwards and forwards, backwards and forwards, backwards and forwards. He wasn't sure if he could remember seeing that other Ricky or not.

Sean struggled to understand. His mind still felt doped. It was temporal shock, the effect of the shunt plus the effect of the change that had just taken place in the very recent past with Ricky's arrival there. The past would be constantly changing with each swing of the pendulum. The robot experiments had shown that. Each swing and they'd all have an entirely new set of memories, reaching back further and further, five minutes, fifty minutes, five hundred minutes, five thousand minutes....

Something was glowing now on the far wall.

The temporal energy must be building up again, creating displacement momentum for the next shunt. They had said the swings were going to be quick ones in the early stages of the journey, in and out of the past or the future in just a couple of minutes during the first few shunts, zip zip zip zip.

Dr White said, 'There's nothing to worry about, Sean. It's all going to work out all right.'

Sean nodded and smiled. Suddenly his mind seemed to clear a little. He was beginning to feel like himself again. 'Sure it will,' he said. 'I never doubted it.' He became aware of a strangeness beginning to enfold him. The field was taking him onwards. 'Say hello to Ricky for me,' he said, and waved at them as they grew blurry around him. 'I'll see you all a little later.'

3

Eric + 50 minutes

He was falling. Like Alice going down the rabbit hole, except that when she fell it was in a slow, stately way, with plenty of time to look around. He was plummeting crazily, a wild juggernaut zooming through the centre of the earth. Down through the geological strata, past the Cretaceous and the Jurassic, past the Permian, the Silurian, the Cambrian. Choking and gasping, tumbling end over end, arms and legs flailing, his hair flying in the hot breeze that came blasting up from below.

He thought he was going to fall forever.

He had never imagined it was possible to feel so sick and dizzy.

'All the worst stuff comes right at the beginning,' Sean had told him. 'And then it's okay.'

Had Sean really said that? Eric tried to remember. Yes. It was at the minus-fifty-minute level, just when he and Sean were both starting to get a little panicky about the crazy project they had committed themselves to. And then

Sean$_2$ had come whistling out of the future looking cocky and cheerful. Engaging in a whole bunch of incomprehensible babble with Dr Ludwig about how past tense and future tense lose their meanings when you travel in time. And then, jaunty as can be, coming over to Eric and Sean, to tell them not to worry about anything.

'It's all going to be fine. Just let yourself go, and don't try to fight it,' he had said.

Sure, Sean.

Down and down and down. Did *you* fall like this, Sean, when you made *your* first jump into the future? Down, down, down through the primordial rock of the earth into the bubbling volcanic magma at the core of the planet.

Eric wondered when it was going to stop. And what it was going to feel like when he hit bottom.

Then he realized that he was floating rather than dropping. And then that he wasn't even floating. He was still in the laboratory, not in some tunnel that passed through the bowels of the earth. That falling sensation had been just in his imagination, a side effect of the trip forwards in time. In fact his feet were firmly planted on the floor of the shunt platform.

So he had arrived. He was fifty minutes in the future.

Everything was a blur. Eric was so dizzy that he thought his head would spin free from his shoulders. And the nausea that he was feeling was terrible.

'Somebody grab me or I'm going to fall,' he managed to blurt out.

They caught him just as he started to go over.

'Easy,' someone said. 'The disorientation lasts only a couple of moments. Going into the future seems to be more traumatic than going into the past.'

'So I notice,' Eric murmured.

But they were right: you did come out of it pretty fast. He was able to stand unaided now. He could focus his eyes again. The digital elapsed-time counter on the rear wall confirmed that he was exactly fifty minutes into the experiment. Right on schedule.

Sean must already have materialized here ahead of him, making the plus-five-minutes shunt. Eric wondered whether Sean had gone through the same awful rabbit-hole sensation then. He wondered whether Sean . . . Sean . . .

Suddenly Eric felt with full force the impact of his twin brother's absence. The strangeness, the aloneness, the separateness.

It came rushing in like a roaring tidal wave: the knowledge that time stood between him and his brother like a sword. He hadn't felt it on his first time-jump, because that had been a backwards one, and when he arrived he had seen Sean right there in the lab, getting ready to begin the experiment. But at this very moment Sean was a hundred minutes away, back at the minus-fifty-minute level. The balancing swing of the pendulum, the equal and opposite displacement.

From here to Time Ultimate – the end of the experiment, some ninety-five million years out from the starting point – they were never going to be on the same side of the time-line again. One of them would always be in the minus-time level while the other one was an equal distance up ahead in plus-time.

Eric stepped down from the platform and took a couple of uncertain steps.

'How do you feel now?' Dr White asked.

He managed to smile at her. 'Better.' It was a lie. 'Just a little wobbly. Just a little.'

'It's a jolt, isn't it?'

He nodded. He wanted to ask Sean how *he* had felt on his first forwards jump. But of course Sean wasn't here. It was weird, not having him nearby. Not feeling that odd, almost telepathic bond. The sensation that said, *I am here, I am Sean, I am closer to you than anyone on this planet and always will be.* Almost as if they were Siamese twins and not the ordinary kind. Eric had never talked about that with Sean. It had always seemed, well, embarrassing – telling him what he felt, asking him if he felt it, too. But he was pretty sure that Sean felt it, too.

And right now Eric was feeling the lack of it. Intensely.

'Fifty minutes from Time Zero,' he said. 'I don't suppose much can have changed in the world yet.'

Dr White chuckled. 'Not in fifty minutes. All the really interesting things are still ahead of you.'

'Ahead of me?' Eric shook his head. 'No, you've got it upside down. The way I look at it, all the really interesting stuff's *behind* me.'

She looked baffled by that.

'You don't know what I mean?' he said.

'Well—'

'No, you don't, do you. I'm Eric, remember?'

'Yes, of course, but—' Her voice trailed off.

'The twin who's the paleontologist. The one who's a lot more interested in the past than the future.' He made a broad, sweeping gesture. 'I don't mind getting a peek at the future. But what I'm really waiting for is at the other end of the pendulum. The Mesozoic, back there at the end of the whole circus. The dinosaurs!' He felt heat rising in his cheeks. Excitement coursing through him, making his heart pound. 'That's why I volunteered for this crazy ride, don't you know? To meet the dinosaurs, face to face. It's as simple as that. To walk up to a live dinosaur and say hello.'

4

Sean – 50 minutes

It was different this time, the second shunt. Sean didn't feel that initial sense of dead calmness that had tricked him before into thinking he hadn't gone anywhere. Nor was there a rush of confusion and bewilderment and dismay right afterwards. Instead he felt only a second or two of mild dizziness, and then everything seemed fine.

Maybe it's only the first shunt that's the worst, he thought. Or maybe it's easier because this time I went backwards in time instead of forwards.

He looked around the lab.

They were all running back and forth like a bunch of lunatics, getting all the last-minute stuff ready. The experiment would happen in less than an hour. So there they were, hooking things up, checking circuits, crunching numbers. There was Dr Ludwig, face shiny with sweat, yelling into a pocket telephone. And Dr White, who was usually so calm and gentle, practically tearing at her hair. Harrell, the maths man, was working at two computers at once. Other scientific types were frenziedly doing other

22

final-hour things. And the technicians zipping around the way people did in the ancient silent movies, going much too fast and moving in a silly jerky way.

The only people who looked calm were Ricky and Sean, those intrepid Gabrielson boys. They were standing off to one side with a numbed, dazed look on their faces, waiting to be told to mount the shunt platform and sit down on either side of the displacement torus.

It all looked terribly familiar. Sean had lived through this scene once, after all, less than an hour ago. Now here he was again. Only this time he wasn't waiting around to be told to sit down on the platform. That was those two fellows over there. He was somebody else, $Sean_2$, the traveller in time, the man from fifty minutes in the future.

'Hey,' he said. 'Over here. Me. Anybody going to say hello to me?'

There was a sudden stunned silence in the room. They had all been so busy running through the final insane setting-up procedures that they hadn't even noticed him materialize. But they noticed him now.

'The second backswing!' someone cried. 'Here he is!'

'Absolutely,' Sean said. 'The big surprise. The walking, talking paradox man. You've never seen anything like me, right? You don't remember seeing any of us heading backwards before, is that it?'

'Not yet,' replied Dr Ludwig. His voice sounded thick and hoarse. He looked a little dazed, as though perhaps he hadn't been fully prepared for what was happening. Even he, who had spent years thinking about these concepts while he was planning the experiment. 'You are the first, but of course not the last. Others will come before you, but we do not remember them yet. You are Sean, yes? Making your second shunt, the minus-fifty-minute swing. But soon there will be Eric at minus five hundred minutes, coming in yesterday evening.'

Sean laughed. ' "There *will* be Eric, coming in yesterday evening"? I like the way you say that.'

'We will come to remember his visit, yes, after he has made it. We will need an entirely new grammar to speak of these things. Past tense and future tense lose their meanings when cause and effect are broken free from all mooring. You understand what I am saying?'

'Absolutely,' Sean said.

On this shunt all of it made perfect sense to him. How different from his experience at plus five minutes, when fog was so thick in his brain! Thank God his mind was working right again. It had been scary to think he might have been rendered stupid forever by his trip through time.

It wasn't logical, of course, that this retroactive re-arrangement of the past should happen in stages. With everyone's memories of the hours and days just prior to Time Zero being altered again and again, each time a wider swing brought a new Eric or a Sean back to some point earlier than the last one.

Logically all such changes in the past should occur at once. From the moment the final switch was thrown, there *would always have been* Erics and Seans scattered all up and down the time-stream across the whole span of the experiment's 190 million years.

But there wasn't anything logical about time travel in the first place. Sean knew. It gloriously defied all the laws of cause and effect. And so evidently each swing of the pendulum was going to produce a completely new version of the past. Reality would be fluid from now on, and no one within that shifting reality would ever be aware of the changes. They could never remember the past as it used to be. The moment the change was made, the past would always have been the way it was now.

Only he and Eric, the daring young men on the flying

24

trapeze, moving as outside observers, would be able to comprehend the havoc they were wreaking as they flashed back and forth across the fabric of time, reweaving it as they went. And even they would start to lose track of the changes as the paradoxes mounted.

He walked over to Eric and Sean$_1$. God, they looked pale and sweaty! That was embarrassing. They were really nervous. He didn't remember having felt that nervous himself when it had been his turn to be Sean$_1$, fifty minutes ago. He thought of himself as having waited calmly, coolly and confidently for his launching into the time-shunt.

But he realized that he was probably kidding himself. The way Sean$_1$ looked now was the way he himself must have looked fifty minutes ago, because he had been Sean$_1$ then. There was no hiding from the truth of that. He had been scared stiff. Fifty minutes ago he had been sitting there waiting to be converted into a cluster of tachyons — particles that move faster than light and travel backwards in time in an anti-time universe. What the singularity coupling did was turn him into a tachyonic replica of himself, throwing off showers of anti-time energy that would be exactly balanced by the time-force liberated in the opposite direction. At least that was what it was supposed to do. And he had been sitting there wondering if it would.

Well, it had. And here he was.

They were staring goggle-eyed at him. As though he had no business being there. As though he was some evil being who had come to haunt the place.

Sean smiled.

'Relax,' he said. 'It's all going to be fine. Just let yourself go, and don't try to fight it. You won't like it at first, but all the worst stuff comes right at the beginning, and then it's okay.'

A little comfort, a little friendly cheer. It was the least he

25

could do for them, he thought. For Ricky. And also for Sean$_1$, who was sitting there looking so pale and miserable. His brother and his other self. If there's anyone in the world who's closer and dearer to you than your twin brother, Sean thought, it's your other self.

5

Eric − 5×10^2 minutes

The big room was oddly peaceful, here on the night before the experiment. It was about two in the morning. The overhead lights were turned off, and the only illumination came from a couple of green security lamps off to the side.

Nobody seemed to be there when Eric stepped off the shunt platform after a moment of arrival vertigo blessedly more brief than it had been the last time. He looked around. Nobody here at all? That was peculiar. They knew what time he'd be due to arrive on this swing. Even if most of them would be asleep at this hour, resting up for the big day ahead of them tomorrow, *somebody* should have been here to debrief him when he showed up.

Then he noticed one of the younger scientists – a quasi-conductor man named John Terzunian – dozing in the darkness.

Eric went over to him and touched him gently on the shoulder.

'Johnny? Johnny, wake up. It's me, Eric, making the

minus-five-hundred-minute shunt.'

'What? Who?' A look of sudden panic. 'Oh, God, I must have dropped off.'

'Happens to anyone,' Eric said. The other man looked hardly older than he was, maybe twenty-five, twenty-six, barely past his doctorate. His hair was thinning already. His eyes were jet black and very bloodshot. 'Don't worry. I won't tell. Everyone else is asleep, huh?'

Terzunian nodded. 'The last one left an hour ago. We drew lots for who would stay till you came in.'

'And you lost.'

A sheepish smile. 'Nobody's had much sleep for three or four nights in a row, now. I wouldn't mind being in bed right this minute. But somebody had to be here to meet you.'

'Sure,' Eric said. 'I understand.'

He thought of $Sean_1$ and $Eric_1$, snoring away in the dorm section a couple of hundred yards from the lab. For them, he knew, edginess had fought a battle with exhaustion and exhaustion had won.

Well, it was a good idea for them to be sleeping. This would be the last chance they'd have to get a proper night's sleep in the year 2016 for a long time to come. Little more than eight hours from now they were going to set out on a journey that would carry them some ninety-five million years in each direction before they saw their own home year again. Adrift in the time-stream, swinging back and forth, swooping through the eons.

It was strange, thinking of $Sean_1$ and $Eric_1$ as *them* instead of *us*. But he had to. Those two guys sleeping down there in the dorm weren't Sean and Eric Gabrielson at all, not really. Not to him. They were two entirely separate people: $Sean_1$ and $Eric_1$. Yesterday's selves. They hadn't yet begun to oscillate in time. They still had no real idea of what any of this was going to be like.

To them, if they thought of him at all, he would be $Eric_2$, an Eric of the future, tomorrow's Eric, an unreal Eric. That was all right. He didn't feel unreal. He wasn't living in tomorrow. He was living in *now*. It was a now that kept sliding around between past and future, but all the same it was the only now he had. He was real enough to himself: the true and authentic Eric. And the true and authentic Sean, for him, was the one who was nearly seventeen hours away just now, up there at the plus-500-minute level, at the opposite end of the time-travel seesaw that they were riding.

Everything was in balance. Everything was symmetrical.

It all had the intense bright clarity of a very powerful dream. Except that it was actually happening to them, and it would go on happening for something like ninety-five million years.

Terzunian asked, 'Can I get you anything? A drink of water? Something to eat?'

'No, thanks,' Eric said. 'So far as subjective time goes, this is still just the beginning of the experiment for me. I've only experienced a few minutes of elapsed time since the whole thing started.'

'All right,' Terzunian said. 'We'd better get down to work, then. I'm supposed to ask you questions about your psychological and physical state upon arrival. Here – the camera's on. Testing. Testing.' He seemed twitchy, ill at ease, afraid of messing anything up. Well, Eric thought, he's been involved with this project for years, and now here it is, actually happening.

Actually happening. Yes.

There were times when he had trouble believing that he and Sean had really agreed to do it. Of course they had known about the experiment for years – Project Pendulum had got under way when they were still in high school, as soon as the development of artificially produced

29

minisingularities had provided the technological basis for travelling in time.

Sean had brought home a pile of theoretical papers about it. Explaining how the phase-linkage coupling of a minute black hole, identical to those that are found all over interstellar space, and its mathematical opposite, a 'white hole', created an incredibly powerful force that ripped right through the fabric of space-time – and how that force could be contained and controlled, like a bomb in a basket, so that it could be used as a transit tube for making two-way movements in time.

Eric's first reaction on hearing that was to imagine himself running backwards along the earth's geological history as if seeing a film from back to front – soaring through the epochs, past the Pleistocene and the Pliocene into the days of the dinosaurs, the early amphibians, the trilobites, back even to the primordial days when there was nothing on the surface of the world except a bare granite shield rising above a steaming sea. Tremendous! To see it all. Not to have to reconstruct it from compressed strata and scattered fossils, but to look at everything with your own eyes while it still existed.

His second reaction was to think that the whole notion was completely crazy, a fantastic pipe dream.

No, Sean had said. It really can work. Here, let me show you the equations.

And Sean had scribbled equations for him until he begged for mercy. Maths on Sean's level was a mysterious language to him, as remote and inaccessible as the language the ancient Egyptians spoke in their dreams. The more Sean explained it, the less Eric understood – or cared. But Sean was convinced that the theory of time-shunting was correct, and Sean was usually right about anything he investigated with such passion. At least in the world of physics.

That's extraordinary, Eric had said, figuring that fifty or sixty years of solid work would be necessary, at the very least, before time travel was anything more than a set of fascinating equations. And then he put it all totally out of his mind. He had other things to think about that seemed more urgent, like going to college, and his graduate work in paleontology after that.

But then came news that the first displacement machine had actually been built and tested. Eric paid some mild attention to that. Robots equipped with data-recording gear and cameras went off, so it was claimed, on safaris in time. The robots made their journey and returned to the same instant from which they had been sent off. To the watching scientists the elapsed time of the experiment was zero. So there was no way of telling that anything had happened, except for the power drain that the instrument measured – and except for the paradoxes.

The paradoxes! Even though the robots hadn't seemed to go anywhere, they turned up in the laboratory hours and days and weeks before they had been sent out. That gave everyone headaches, thinking about it. The past kept flowing and shifting around, and nobody's memory was a safe place: things were always getting different from what you thought and remembered.

And the robots also turned up an equal number of hours and days and weeks *after* the experiment, flashing suddenly into existence in the laboratory and staying around for a few minutes, maybe an hour or two, before vanishing again.

The robots seemed to have suffered no ill effects from their mysterious journeys. They appeared still to be in fine working order. But the cameras they carried yielded nothing but fogged film. Sean explained that film emulsion was evidently unable to withstand the tachyon storms to which it was exposed during the time-shunts. The data-recording gear had produced scrambled digital read-outs, just static, probably for the same reason.

Oh, Eric had said. Tachyon storms, is that so?

He didn't bother asking for more elaborate explanations. Not then.

They sent living creatures through the machine, too – turtles, frogs and rabbits. The usual nature organizations complained about that, but the animals all came back safely. Back from where? Who could say? No question that they had gone *somewhere.* The usual time-displacement paradoxes had been observed: rabbits popping out of nowhere in the laboratory three days before the start of the experiment, and doing the same thing three days after the experiment, too.

That was interesting, a remarkable achievement. If the rabbits could be sent three days backwards and forwards in time, they might well have gone a million years, or fifty million. Still, what could a turtle or a rabbit tell anybody about the way the Mesozoic really looks, or the world of AD 1,000,000? You could send a turtle to the end of time and back, and it wouldn't give you one syllable of useful information about its trip.

So of course they called for volunteers.

Human time travellers would have to go through the machine in order to get any significant results. Only a lunatic, Eric figured, would volunteer for a deal like that.

The word went out that they wanted to use a pair of identical twins, because there had to be an exact balance of momentum down to the last milligram. Twins, because they had the same bone structure and pretty much the same distribution of body fat, would make it that much easier to attain that balance.

That's nice, Eric thought. And went back to his doctoral thesis on Arctic amphibian life in the Mesozoic period.

They're looking for twins with scientific background, someone told him.

Eric simply shrugged.

Ideally they want one twin who's a physicist and one who's a paleontologist, someone else told him. In order to maximize the value of their observations.

Right. Eric was a paleontologist. Sean was a physicist.

That's very interesting, Eric said, still showing no interest at all. I suppose we're not the only twins who meet that requirement. They'll find someone sooner or later who'll be willing to risk the trip.

Then one day Sean turned up and said, 'Don't you think it could help your research a little if you got to look at some *living* Mesozoic creatures, Ricky?'

And now here he was five hundred minutes in his own past, locked into an unstoppable series of ever-widening swings in time, back and forth, back and forth, minutes and hours and months and years and centuries and eons. Like a dream, a very strange and intense dream, a dream brighter and sharper than any reality he had ever experienced.

'Go ahead,' Terzunian said. 'This is the minus-five-hundred minute level, John Terzunian speaking. Eric Gabrielson has just arrived right on schedule: the third backswing.' He pointed at Eric to give him his cue. 'Okay. Make your report.'

'There's not a lot to tell. Easy arrival, none of the queasiness I felt when I made the minus-five-minute shunt. Just a fast flicker of discomfort, then everything normal. Some minor spatial displacement: I came in a couple of feet to the left of my departure point. No fatigue so far. Maybe some mild uneasiness – no, uneasiness is too strong a word, a little edginess, maybe ....'

Terzunian was staring at him. There was a peculiar

expression on his face that seemed to be a mixture of fascination and envy and what might have been something like pity.

'Well, look,' Eric said, 'there really isn't anything to report yet. Give me another few shunts and I'll have plenty to say. *Plenty.*'

But who will I say it to, he wondered? When I'm nine and a half years in the past? Or 950,000 years in the future?

6

Sean $+ 5 \times 10^2$ minutes

This time it felt as if some giant had scooped him up, popped him into a slingshot and whirled him around, and tossed him with all his might. When he landed, the sides of the laboratory were circling around him like the rim of a big centrifuge and the floor was rocking wildly from side to side. The place might just as well have been a carnival funhouse. Sean flung himself down flat, hanging on for all he was worth.

But the effect lasted only a minute or two. The wild funhouse gyrations slowed down and then they stopped altogether. He patted the floor to make certain it had finished moving. Apparently it had. He got to his feet carefully, steadying himself with his outstretched arms. He took two or three cautious steps. Everything was holding still, now. Fine. Fine.

'It takes a little getting used to,' he said to nobody in particular.

He looked around. There were new changes in the

laboratory. He was five hundred minutes in the future: eight hours and twenty minutes since the start of the experiment. Night had fallen. The fluorescent lights seemed harsher and brighter. The big room was weirdly quiet, almost ominous.

'Tell us what you experienced,' Dr Ludwig said.

Dr Ludwig and Dr White were the only people in the room. The technicians must have been sent home. The shunt platform was strangely forlorn and abandoned with no one around it. The two metal seats that flanked the displacement cone might have been nothing more than a couple of classroom chairs. The cone itself seemed trivial, a mere chunk of inactive machinery.

Staring at it, Sean had trouble believing that under that glossy lump of shielding lurked a symmetrical pair of laboratory-generated collapsed stars: a miniature black hole and its mirror image, a so-called white hole. Together they made up a pair of perfectly balanced singularities – zones of strangeness where nothing behaved according to the rules of the ordinary universe – held in an unbreakable coupling. Infinite energy forever circled in a loop between the interlocked event horizons of those singularities. Energy that had opened the time gate through which Sean and Eric had been shunted to begin their immense voyage through time and anti-time.

Dr Ludwig's eyes looked bleary and his plump cheeks were dark with stubble. It was the look of a man who has been in the office too long. When Sean had made his last trip through here at plus five minutes – hardly any time at all ago for Sean, eight hours and twenty minutes for them – Dr Ludwig had been pink and freshly shaven.

'The first time,' Sean said, 'I thought I was losing my mind. The first forward swing, the plus-five-minutes one. Let me tell you, it was a truly hideous experience.'

'The forward swings are worse than the backward ones?' Dr White asked.

'So it seems. All that disorientation and mental fog, the sheer *stupidity* that I felt. The first backward swing, the minus-fifty-minutes one, was a little jarring, but nothing like that. And the disturbance only lasted for a moment.'

'And this time? The second forward swing?'

'Dizziness, really serious dizziness, everything whirling like mad. But not as strong as the first time and it didn't last nearly as long.'

'Yet it was stronger than what you felt on the one backswing you've made so far?'

Sean nodded. 'It's as though there's some real effort in making the forward swings, something that demands a lot from you in breaking free of the time fabric. Whereas when you go the other way you slide along the track pretty easily, and there's just the slightest little disturbance.'

'Perhaps so,' Dr Ludwig said. 'But we have reasons to think that the shunt effects in both directions will diminish the further you get from Time Zero.'

Sean grinned. 'They'd better. We're not going to be landing in this nice safe lab many more times, are we?' The pendulum swings were going to be getting wider and wider. Sudden visions blazed in his mind: the dark steamy past, the shimmering unimaginable future. 'It'll be nice not to get an attack of the dizzies every time we arrive,' he said. 'In some of the places where we're going to turn up we may need to hit the ground running.'

7

Eric $+ 5 \times 10^3$ minutes

'If nobody minds very much,' Eric said, 'I'd like to have a quick look at today's newspaper before I shuffle along towards last month.'

The elapsed-time counter in front of him read 83.33 hours. Which was just short of three and a half days since Time Zero. And so this ought to be Friday night, the twenty-second of April.

He saw them exchanging glances. Was it okay to give him a paper? They weren't sure. Someone on the psychology staff went off to ask Dr Ludwig, and apparently the answer was yes, because he came back with a newspaper in his hands.

It was a fresh printout and had that brand-new smell of newsprint. Eric stared at the date.

Friday 22 April 2016.

So it really was true. He was actually travelling in time.

Unless this was all some crazy hoax – some kind of psychological experiment, maybe? And they had given him a paper with a phony date, so that he'd be fooled into believing—

That's paranoid thinking, Ricky-boy, he told himself. All this is *real*. You'd better believe it.

He glanced quickly over the front-page stories. Tenth anniversary of lunar settlement celebrated here and on the moon. The President's visit to Antarctica. An earthquake in Turkey, 6.3 on the Richter scale, exactly as predicted last month. A big feature at the bottom of the page about the Robot Pride Day parade in Detroit, fifty thousand mechanical workers taking part.

He didn't see any story about the time-travel experiment now under way at Cal Tech.

But it would have surprised him if he had. The whole project was classified data, partly because the government wanted it that way and partly because a lot of people were scared stiff of the whole idea of time travel. The response to the earliest announcements of the project had been unexpectedly heated. Certain historians and philosophers had argued that there might be irreparable damage to contemporary life if the past was changed in any way by time travellers. One small alteration – the plucking of a flower, the squashing of a bug – might wipe out whole empires, for all anyone knew. Then, too, some religious leaders were troubled by the possibility that visitors to the past might discover that scriptural history was inaccurate in some way. And there were always those people who feared any new development in science, especially one as startling and magical as this. So it had been decided on the highest levels not to release any details of Project Pendulum until there had been a chance to study the effects of the first few shunts.

Turning to the sports pages, Eric saw that the Dodgers had just dropped their third straight game in Osaka after losing two out of three in Honolulu. The new baseball season wasn't starting off very promisingly. Things were doing a little better for the local basketball team: the Lakers had won their play-off series against Buenos Aires and were now going on to play Nairobi for the championship.

The weather for the Pasadena area was going to be fair and warm. It had rained in San Francisco yesterday but the storm wasn't expected to reach Southern California. The stock market had had a good day, the Dow Jones averages rising 112 points to 7786. Eric felt curiously superstitious about looking at the obituary page and went past it quickly, averting his eyes.

'Here,' he said, handing the paper back. 'Thanks.'

'How does it feel?'

Eric grinned. 'I always like to see Friday's newspaper on Tuesday,' he said. 'You get a good jump on things that way.'

8

Sean − 5×10^3 minutes

Four of them were waiting for him on the next swing: Dr White and Dr Thomas representing the psychological side of the experiment, Dr Mukherji and Dr Camminella representing the theoretical mathematicians.

This was his fourth shunt. It was beginning to mount up now. The swings were calibrated in logarithmically increasing intervals, each one ten times wider than the one before. So he had gone five minutes into the future, then fifty minutes into the past, five hundred minutes into the future, five thousand minutes into the past . . . .

Five thousand minutes. Five times 10^3 minutes. Five thousand minutes was 83 hours and 20 minutes, which was 3.46 days. Time Zero for the experiment, the point from which all the shunting began, was Tuesday 19 April 2016, at half-past ten in the morning. And here he was, stepping down from the shunt platform three and a half days before that.

The reception committee seemed to be having a little

trouble coming to terms with that. They were all trying had to look cool and collected. Sean could see them working at it.

But they didn't even come close to being able to hide their amazement. Their eyes were wide, their faces were flushed, their tongues kept licking back and forth over dry lips. It was the look of people who knew that they were experiencing something miraculous.

'Nice of you all to be here to greet me,' he said cheerfully. 'I'm Sean, in case you weren't quite certain. It's last Friday night, isn't it?'

'Friday, yes,' Dr White said. Her voice was thick and husky, choked with emotion. 'The fifteenth of April.'

'At eleven-ten p.m.,' said Sean. 'On the button.'

'On the button,' Dr White said.

Why did they seem so stunned? After all, this was his fourth shunt, two forward and now two back. They ought to be getting used to it by now.

Then he scowled at his own idiocy. *He* was getting used to it. But it was all new to these people. They were living three and a half days ago, back there before the start of the experiment. This was the first time they were seeing a shunter.

Maybe they had never truly believed the experiment would work. Or maybe they accepted it on a theoretical level but hadn't properly prepared themselves for the real thing — for having him come dropping right out of next Tuesday like this. Despite all the years they had put in, working towards this moment, thinking about what it was going to be like to make time travel an actuality, his arrival must be an overpowering, almost shattering event for them.

Dr Thomas said, 'We have a few tests that we'd like you to take.'

Sean gave him a sour look. 'Tests?'

42

Dr Thomas was the team's head psychologist, and he was *always* saying, 'We have a few tests we'd like you to take.' Sean had never cared much for the trim, smug little psychologist, who sometimes seemed more like a computerized simulation of a human being than an actual flesh and blood person.

In the planning stages of the project he had subjected Sean and Eric to multiphasic electronic devices that buzzed and flashed and screeched maddeningly as they probed the twins' minds. The ordeal was necessary, they were told, to find out whether they were stable enough to withstand the stress of time-shunting. Apparently they were.

All right. What more did Thomas need to know now? The biggest test of all was under way this very minute: the experiment itself. Wasn't that enough for him? Sean hadn't been expecting another bout with those instruments of torture.

'Over here, please,' Dr Thomas said. 'Can you walk unaided?'

'Of course I can walk unaided. You think I've become brain-damaged?'

'Please. There isn't much time.'

'I simply wonder why it's necessary to inflict even more of these idiotic—'

'What we wish to determine,' Dr Thomas said frostily, 'is whether retrograde motion through time has injurious effects on the human nervous system. Or, if you prefer me to put it in words of a single syllable—'

'You wouldn't know how to,' Sean said. 'But I assure you that my mind is still working properly. I could even spell "retrograde" for you. Maybe even "injurious". How about "retrograde" backwards? That would be E-D-A-R-G—'

Dr White put her hand lightly over Sean's and said very quietly, 'We don't have any doubt that you're taking the shunt beautifully, Sean. But we do need quantitative data.

43

We have to know things about your pulse rate, your reaction times, your automatic reflexes, etcetera, etcetera. It really is important. And this is practically our only chance to get it. The testing machines are set up to record everything quickly and automatically. We've only got fifteen minutes, you know, before you go shunting off again into the future.'

Throughout the entire life of the project Dr White had been the cool, gentle voice of reason. Whenever anyone had started yelling – and there had been plenty of that, as deadlines neared and everybody's nerves grew taut – she had always been the one to restore peace.

Once again Sean found it impossible to resist her calm, easy manner. With a sigh he said, 'All right, go ahead and test me.'

He waited grimly for the onslaught of the blinking screens and whirling patterns and screaming sirens. Might as well humour them, he thought. Dr White was right when she said that they wouldn't have many more chances to do this to him. The next time he came backwards, it would be at the minus-5 x 10^5-minutes level. That would be nearly a year ago. They probably would be expecting him then, and they'd have more tests ready. But the swing after that would bring him into the past at minus 5 x 10^7 minutes. That would be the year 1921. Dr Thomas wouldn't even have been born then, neither would his parents. Maybe not even Dr Thomas's grandparents. He wasn't going to have to worry about Dr Thomas or anybody else sitting him down in front of multiphasic testing machines in the year 1921.

9

Eric − 5×10^4 minutes

It was raining. Eric could hear the drumbeat of the drops hitting the roof of the single-storey laboratory building.

So this had to be March. The month before the experiment. It had rained practically every day in March, a torrential climax to the wettest winter Southern California had had in years, causing mudslides and other calamities all over the place. Then at the end of the month the sun had reappeared, and the weather had been dry and warm ever since, as it probably was going to be until autumn. There is hardly ever any rain in Southern California between April and November. But plenty of it was coming down right now.

The sound of the rain was beautiful in his ears. Maybe hillsides were turning to muck and goo out there and houses were floating off their foundations, but to Eric the pounding of those pelting drops was the sweetest music he could imagine. It told him that everything was still going according to plan.

He was fifty thousand minutes in the past. That was 833.3 hours. Or 34.72 days. They had drilled the arithmetic of the time journey into him until he could recite it in his sleep.

You jumped ten times as far on each shunt as on the one before. But you alternated a swing to the future with one to the past, so each time you returned to the past you landed a hundred times further back than you had on the last jump. The same with the future. The early swings were very close together, but the hundred-fold factor kept multiplying.

So it was 8.33 hours back, and 83.3 hours forward, and then 833.3 hours back, and 8333.3 hours forward, and then 83,333.3 hours back, which worked out to 9.51 years into the past. Then 91.13 years forward. And then 951.3 years back. Then 9,513 years forward. And then 95,129.3 years back. And then 951,293.7 years forward. Then 9,512,937.5 years back. And then—

And then the top of the pendulum swing, the swing to Time Ultimate, the effective limit of the experiment at which point he would have been carried some ninety-five million years into the future and then an equal distance back – back to the Cretaceous Period – back to the time of the dinosaurs.

He listened joyfully to the beat of the rain. Thinking: yes, carry me back, carry me back, let me look upon the dawn of time.

'Eric?' a voice said.

'Right the first try.'

'Do you know what day this is?'

'Wednesday 16 March 2016.'

'Yes. Yes, that's right. And what day is it for you?'

'Just a little bit past Time Zero. Tuesday, the nineteenth of April. At not quite eleven a.m.'

They were staring at him that way that was getting to be

46

so tiresomely familiar to him – staring as if they were looking at a ghost. Dr Ludwig, Dr White, Dr Thomas, Dr Mukherji, Dr Camminella, and half a dozen more. The whole crew. They had a pale winter-time look about them and they were wearing heavier clothes than they had on when he had seen them a little while ago at Time Zero.

The lab was different, too. Everything was raw and half-finished. Electrical conduits dangled in mid-air. The displacement cone was unshielded and the singularity cradles lay open and empty. Crates and cartons were scattered all about, still unpacked. A month and three days to go and they still had a ton of work to do, getting everything set up. But of course they were going to finish the job on schedule. There wasn't any doubt of that. His being here now was the proof of that.

The March rain drummed down in double time.

'If you don't mind,' Dr Thomas said. 'There are some tests that we'd like to administer—'

10

Sean + 5×10^4 minutes

'I know you're all waiting to stick the electrodes on my head and measure everything that's going on inside it,' Sean said. 'But would it be okay if I stepped out into the fresh air for a moment? I've still got a headache from the *last* batch of tests.'

'Still?' Dr Thomas asked. 'That was a month ago!'

'A month ago for you people, yes. For me the lights and bells are still blasting away.'

'Well, I suppose – for just a few minutes.'

'Don't worry. I won't try to escape.'

There was a little forced laughter at that. Even so, Terzunian and Mukherji went with him on his little excursion outside the lab. To look after him? Or to make sure he didn't bolt off into the night, fleeing Thomas and his dreaded multiphasic machines to enjoy a couple of hours of solitary jogging through the darkness?

It was gorgeous outside. The air was warm and sweet and gentle, and very clear. The moon was bright and the stars were sparkling. The vines on the laboratory's west wall were in bloom, great yellow flowers filling the air with a wondrous fragrance. This was late May, one of the best months of the year, before the worst of the summer heat and the summer smog descended on the San Gabriel Valley.

He thought of poor Eric, back there in rainy March right at this moment, and smiled.

'Okay,' he said, filling his lungs as deeply as he could. 'I guess I can face those tests now.'

11

Eric + 5×10^5 minutes

The drumbeat sound of the rain ceased between one moment and the next. It was cut off sharply and suddenly, as if an audiotape had been abruptly sliced. Now Eric heard the chirping of birds and the chattering of grasshoppers instead. The warm golden brightness of a perfect Southern California afternoon came bursting in upon him with startling impact.

He realized that he had made another jump. He must be almost a year in the future this time. Half a million minutes beyond Time Zero – 347.2 days. This was March also, but March of a different year, March of 2017.

And he had landed outside the laboratory, on a broad lawn at the far west side of the campus. The time displacement was big enough now that some spatial displacement was occurring also. There were students all around him but nobody seemed to notice his arrival. Or care. Maybe by March of 2017 it was a common thing for time travellers to pop into being here and there around the campus.

Eric felt a heady sense of freedom. He was outdoors in the fresh air, away from Dr Ludwig and the rest of the Project Pendulum crowd, for the first time in – what? weeks? months? All that endless training, testing, rehearsing – he had felt like a cat in a cage, going around and around and around. But there were no Project Pendulum people anywhere in sight now. For however many hours it was until his next shunt, he could go where he pleased, do as he liked.

'Watch it!' someone yelled.

A gravity rotor came skimming by, zigzagging wildly up and down just above eye level. A tall, skinny undergraduate was running alongside it, trying to catch a ride. Eric got out of the way just in time. The student made a desperate lunge and grabbed the rotor just before it went lurching out of reach. It carried him a hundred yards or so through the air until it lost its spin and fluttered to the ground.

A pang of nostalgia went through Eric. It seemed like a million years since he had played with gravity rotors as a student on this same campus, though actually it was no more than three or four years ago.

Soon, he thought with a little shiver, he *would* be almost a million years away from his college days. And then a great deal more than that.

A slender blonde girl keyed up the rotor again and let it fly. As it began to circle the lawn, Eric found himself suddenly loping after it. There were half a dozen students chasing it too, but he brushed them aside with a quick gesture. Easily, gracefully, he reached up and slipped his hands into the rotor's holdfasts and let it spin him upward and outward across the campus. He had always been good with gravity rotors. He knew how to play into their axis of rotation so they would take him on a maximum glide. Up – up –

'Eric! Eric, have you gone crazy!' a hoarse, angry voice

was shouting, far below.

He laughed and waved.

'Come down from there, you lunatic! What do you think you're doing?'

'Having some fun,' he called, breathless with laughter.

Then he looked down. Half a dozen grim-faced Project members were waving their arms widely at him. As he went spinning past them, fifteen feet over their heads, he caught sight of Dr Thomas, Dr Mukherji, Terzunian, and a few others, staring at him in shock. Dr Ludwig was running towards them from the general direction of the laboratory.

Regretfully he guided the gravity rotor into a downspin and rode it to a landing.

'What kind of absurd stunt was that?' Dr Ludwig blurted. 'Suppose you had broken your neck! What would happen to the Project then?'

Eric smiled. 'I wouldn't have been hurt,' he said serenely. 'It's impossible. How could anything happen to me? I'm not really here, remember? I'm still back there at Time Zero sitting on the shunt platform. And at an infinite number of other places between there and Time Ultimate, all at once. So what's the harm in my taking a little ride?'

'Idiot!' Dr Ludwig blazed. 'Imbecile!' Eric had never seen him so furious. ' *"I'm not really here"*? What are you talking about? Who put such nonsense into your head?'

'The mathematical model—' Eric stammered. 'Sean explained to me that—'

'Sean! That other maniac!' Dr Ludwig clenched his fists and shook them in frustration. In a tightly controlled voice he said, 'Listen to me, Eric, and listen carefully. You are on a pendulum, yes, and you do occupy every point between Time Zero and Time Ultimate. But you can still be harmed at any point in that entire sequence of nearly two hundred million years. And if you are – if you are –' He looked

52

ready to explode. 'The past is fluid! The future is yet unborn! Anything can be changed! Anything! Who knows what will befall the entire history of the world, if anything happens to you? Who knows?'

12

Sean − 5×10^5 minutes

Without warning the mild May night gave way to a glorious May morning – May of the year before. Sean was back in 2015, 347.2 days before the opening of the experiment.

He stood blinking in the sudden sunlight. The shunts were coming much more easily now, causing little or no sense of transition as he shuttled between past and future. He was outside the laboratory. Outside the campus, in fact, half a mile or so east of it in downtown Pasadena. The first significant spatial displacement, he realized. The early shunts had moved him no more than a few inches from his Time Zero position on the shunt platform, but by now the jumps were getting big enough to carry him a fair distance.

Casually he strolled down Colorado Boulevard, heading east.

It surprised him that nobody from the lab was waiting here to meet him when he arrived. Up until now they hadn't allowed him to be alone for a moment. At each of his previous shunts – plus five minutes, minus fifty minutes, plus five hundred minutes, minus five thousand minutes, plus fifty thousand minutes – they had clustered around him as soon as he showed up. Now here he was, half a million minutes in the past and they had left him completely on his own. Why weren't they here?

Then he realized that at this stage of the project, back in May of 2015, he and Eric hadn't even been selected yet to be the experimental subjects. The preliminary screening interviews were still going on, all that interminable testing and questioning and checking.

So as of this moment the Project Pendulum people didn't even know who they were going to be sending on the shunt, let alone what time of day or month their time travellers were going to be turning up in the past. How could they? Time Zero itself had kept getting postponed again and again. The choice of 19 April at half-past ten in the morning as the final day and hour and minute for the departure point hadn't been nailed down until 3 March, just six weeks before the day of the experiment.

And even after they had picked it, the Project people would still have had somehow to send information back to themselves of the year before, notifying themselves that experimental subject Sean Gabrielson was due to be popping out of nowhere in downtown Pasadena at such-and-such a time of the morning on such-and-such a day in May 2015, which would be precisely 347.2 days prior to the beginning of the great time-travel event.

Probably they could have done it by sending off a preliminary shunt carrying a robot with the schedule. Maybe they *should* have done it, on the theory that it was best not to let their time traveller have to fend for himself back here. But Project Pendulum's funds had been running pretty low in the final few weeks. Most likely there hadn't been any slack in the budget for extras like that. So they hadn't been able to send the word to anyone back here in 2015 that he'd be coming this way.

But *he* could.

Sean grinned slyly. He was tempted to saunter over to the Cal Tech campus right now and drop in at the laboratory.

'Hi,' he would say. 'I'm Sean Gabrielson. You're going to pick me next month for the shunt. Let's all take an hour off and go out for some pizza, okay?'

He could do that, sure. But suppose they didn't like his dropping in like that. Suppose it struck them as a cocky show-off sort of thing to do. Suppose they decided to dispense with the Gabrielson twins entirely, and pick a different pair of candidates for the shunt. What then? What would happen to him, back here in 2015? Out like a snuffed candle, that's what. He'd never get to see the far future or the distant past, or anything else. He'd go right back to being a graduate physics student in the year 2016 and he'd have no memory of any of the shunts he'd already experienced, let alone the ones that were still to come.

He didn't want to risk that.

But there *was* something he *could* do. It carried some paradox risk also, but he thought it was relatively safe. And useful, in a manner of speaking. And fun.

He thought back to last year, to the final few weeks before the names of the successful candidates for the shunt were announced. Six different pairs of twins had been in the running. Sean had figured all along that he and Eric had the best shot, because they wanted a physicist and a paleontologist, and he and Eric were the only ones who really fulfilled that requirement. But towards the end he had begun to think that the choice might land on one of the other sets of twins. Those shy Bengali girls, the Chakravarti sisters, maybe. They were mathematicians, but one had some sort of a background in archaeology. They were very, very bright. And, most important of all, they had the backing of their countryman, the Project Pendulum theoretician Dr Mukherji.

Right before the choice was due to be announced, Sean had absolutely convinced himself that it was going to be the Chakravartis. He could already feel the disappointment seeping into his soul, and knew that it would embitter him for the rest of his life. A chance to travel to the ends of time, and it had slipped away from him! For days he could hardly sleep or eat. He was half crazy with tension most of the time, snapping and snarling at everybody.

Well, now that he was back here again at the time when that had been going on, he could spare himself all that anguish, couldn't he? Tell himself not to worry, let himself know that everything was going to turn out fine?

A phone booth loomed before him at the corner of Colorado and Fair Oaks. He stepped inside and pressed his thumb to the identification plate. The telephone asked him for the number he wanted and he gave his own.

'The line is busy,' the telephone told him.

'Break in on him. This is an emergency.'

'One moment, please.'

Then his own voice said irritably. 'All right, but if this is any kind of sales pitch—'

'Don't worry, fellow. It's a legitimate call,' Sean said.

'Who's there?'

'You mean you don't recognize my voice?'

A pause. 'Ricky?'

'Close. Try again.'

'Look, I've got no time for guessing games. I happen to be in the midst of very important—'

'Sure you are. I know that. Listen, stupid, you're talking to Sean Gabrielson.'

'What?'

'Sean$_2$, let's say. I'm just passing through.'

'What?'

'On my way to the year 2025. And then back to 1921.'

'What? What?'

'Maybe you aren't as bright as they say you are, buddy. If all you can do is honk like a duck.'

'Hey, I don't have to listen to this kind of crazy—' came the angry voice from the speaker grille, and then the CONNECTION INTERRUPTED light went on.

'Call him back,' Sean told the phone.

'The line is busy.'

'Break in on him, then.'

'The line is under privacy seal,' said the telephone.

Sean swore and shook his head. 'Tell him it's a family emergency.'

'The line is under privacy seal,' the phone repeated.

'I know that. Doesn't family emergency take priority?'

'The line is under privacy seal,' said the phone once more.

'All right,' Sean grunted. 'Forget it.'

For a moment he considered grabbing a cab and going out to his place near the beach to confront himself face to face. But he decided against it. If Sean$_1$ was so twitchy and strung out that he couldn't figure out who had been calling him, he deserved to go on sweating a little while longer about who was going to get the nod from Project Pendulum. Sure, Sean thought. The hell with him. Let him keep on worrying another few weeks. The dummy. Let him just keep right on worrying.

13

Eric $- 5 \times 10^6$ minutes

He could see the house, halfway down the block on the other side of the street. It looked smaller than he recalled, and the pink stucco badly needed repainting. The big palm tree in front was leaning way over, with its roots pulled halfway out of the ground. The earthquake had done that, he remembered. He could see the earthquake crack along the front wall of the house, too. A raw gully like an open trench ran for a hundred yards down the middle of the street. The quake must have come just a couple of days before. They hadn't had a chance to do much cleaning up yet.

The quake, the big Santa Monica earthquake, had happened right at the beginning of October 2006, his freshman year in high school. So once again the shunt had brought him in smack on target, carrying him back exactly 9.51 years. From April of 2016 to October of 2006 – yes, just right. Here he was, nine and a half years in the past. And actually in his own teenage neighbourhood.

That part of it was hard to believe. The shunt had dumped him down in the middle of Santa Monica, at the corner of Wilshire and Eighteenth. His old territory. No more than a five-minute walk from the house where he and Sean had lived from the time they were ten until they went to college. So of course he had to go over to have a look at it. And maybe to catch a glimpse of his own younger self. Of course.

Now, standing across the street from the pink stucco house, Eric found himself wondering if it was such a hot idea to be poking around in his own past like this. Suddenly it didn't feel really good.

Not just stirring up the earthquake memories – the jolt in the middle of the night, dogs barking, the sound of dishes breaking, frightened people running out into the streets. He would have expected that bringing it all vividly back to mind would be disturbing, and it was.

But what was even more troublesome was simply revisiting the ordinary memories, the routine day-to-day stuff. The world of 2006 looked a lot less glamorous than Eric remembered, earthquake damage aside. Everything seemed shabbier and more seedy than he expected. The shops out on Wilshire, the cars in the streets, the advertising billboards – it was all run-down, and every-thing had a dreary, old-fashioned look.

Would things really be so much sleeker and shinier nine and a half years down the line? Maybe so. Or maybe over the years he had simply polished up his memories until the past had a much brighter gloss in his mind than it ever had had in reality.

And then there was all the other stuff to think about again, the adolescent stuff, the business of crossing the line from boyhood into manhood. The changes happening in his body. The conflicts with Sean – he and Sean were always battling like fiends in those days, the good old sibling rivalry, five times as fierce because they were identical twins. Sean was fifteen minutes older and he liked to make a big deal about that. And then, too, the unfocused ambitions, wanting to do something great when he grew up but not having any idea what it would be. The shy, hesitant encounters with girls. Eric had filed all those things away deep within himself. Now, at twenty-three, he wasn't at all sure he wanted to come face to face with them again. It might be better, he thought, to turn around right now and quickly walk the other way.

But he stayed were he was, watching the little pink house across the street and hoping that nobody was watching him.

The upstairs room on the left was his. A poster was taped in the window, probably the dinosaur poster from the Country Museum. There was a big plaster-of-Paris triceratops on the front lawn too, a pretty crude job but not really awful. The summer he was twelve he had spent a messy few days making that. As far back as he could remember, he had been absolutely nuts about dinosaurs. His ambition was to go out to Wyoming and dig up the biggest one ever found. Sean had laughed at that. 'Sure,' he said. 'They'll call it *Ericosaurus supergigantus.*'

Everybody said it was a phase he was bound to grow out of when he was a little older, but he didn't. Instead he got deeper into it, paleontology and geology, too. He studied the folds and strata of the rocks in which fossils were found, though it was always the fossils themselves that fascinated him the most. He could remember feverishly packing his little collection of trilobites and ammonites into a suitcase in the first terrifying minutes after the earthquake, back here when he was thirteen, so that he wouldn't lose them in case a second shock struck and destroyed the house. And then—

Who's that?

A boy had come out of the house and was standing on the little porch, looking around in wonder and dismay at the earthquake debris in the street. Eric stepped back into the shadows. The boy was short and thin, with straight sandy hair going off wildly in all directions. He had to be thirteen and a half, but to Eric he seemed much younger. His face was smooth and bland-looking and had a strange unfinished look about it.

That must be Sean, Eric thought. No, wait . . .

He wasn't sure. Of all the strange things that had happened to him since the pendulum had begun to swing, this was the strangest, that he should be staring at this boy and not know whether he was seeing his brother or himself. It was absolutely impossible to tell. Time had not yet carved the adult face of this boy out of the raw material of early adolescence. His nose was just a snub and his mouth and lower jaw had that unfinished look. And at this age he and Sean must have looked much more alike than they would later. Perhaps if both twins were standing side by side on the porch, he might be able to guess which one was Eric and which Sean. But as it was he was baffled.

It was almost frightening to have time swallow his identity like that. Simply being a twin is complicated enough. But when you start losing track of which twin you are . . . .

Then the boy came down the three cracked steps to the lawn. Pausing by the plaster-of-Paris triceratops, he grinned and stroked its long crooked horns for a moment in an unmistakably affectionate way. Eric, watching from a distance, grinned also.

No doubt of it now. That boy had to be his own younger self. He felt a shiver go sliding down his spine.

Go on, he told himself. Walk across the street. Introduce yourself to him.

He imagined half a dozen impossible things that he

could say.

'Hi, there. You're not going to believe this, but I'm you of the year 2016, taking part in the first time-travel experiment ever.'

Or: 'I'm here to tell you not to worry about a thing. I know you're uneasy about all sorts of stuff that you know lies ahead of you, but I can guarantee that everything's going to turn out just fine for you when you grow up.'

Or maybe: 'There's going to be a girl named Carla in your junior year of high school who likes you a lot better than she does Sean, but you're going to convince yourself that it's the other way around. You'll be wrong about that. Invite her to the prom before he does.'

Or: 'The winner of this year's World Series will be . . . .'

Or: 'Your friend Charlie Graham is going to invite you to fly to Phoenix for Christmas with him and his family in his father's plane this year. Dad won't let you go. Be absolutely sure you don't do anything to change his mind, because that plane's going to get caught in a freak lightning storm, and . . . .'

Or: 'You and Sean are both going to go to Cal Tech four years from now. People are going to try to talk you into going to Harvard or Stanford instead, because they think you and Sean shouldn't go to the same college. Don't listen to them. Go to Cal Tech, or else you may change your entire future and miss out on the best thing that's ever going to happen to you.'

Or . . . .

But he didn't say any of those things. Instead he stayed on his side of the street and hung back in the shadows, watching his younger self emerge from the yard of the little pink house, peer into the postbox for a moment, pause to pull a huge red flower from the hibiscus bush on the front walk, and go running off towards Wilshire. Eric smiled. He waved at the small retreating figure. And thought: You don't need any special tips on the future, boy. Just do whatever feels right to you. You'll make some mistakes, but that's no crime. And one of these days you'll grow up and you'll be me, and you'll go off on the weirdest wild trip that anybody in the whole history of the human race ever took.

14

Sean + 5×10^6 minutes

He guessed he must be somewhere out to the east of Pasadena, at least twenty-five miles, maybe more – around Azusa, Glendora, Claremont, one of those towns. Definitely east: he could see big mountains off to the north, and he was pretty sure that that was Mount Baldy over there. Certainly there weren't any mountains that size west of Pasadena. And the air had that hot, dry inland quality to it.

Sean wasn't surprised to find himself this far from the laboratory. A time displacement of nine and a half years was bound to move him a sizable distance in space. But going *east* puzzled him. After all, his last jump had been a backshunt and it had brought him out west of the laboratory. It stood to reason that shunting in the opposite direction in time ought to move him in the opposite direction spatially too. But maybe not. Expecting anything about time travel to stand to reason was probably stupid.

For a moment he wondered whether he had actually gone backwards in time, not forwards, on this shunt, which might explain the eastward displacement.

No. Impossible. Don't be stupid. The one thing that did make sense in all this shunting was the mathematics of reciprocity. Everything had to balance. You swung back, then you swung forwards, while your brother at the opposite end of the seesaw made an equal and opposite journey. The last place Sean had been was the minus- 5×10^5-minutes level. Now he had to be at the plus-5×10^6-minutes level. There were no two ways about that. Beyond any doubt, he must have gone forwards. His location in time right now, he knew, had to be late November of the year 2025.

In any case he didn't need a computer to tell him that he had moved into the future. One quick look at his surroundings was all that it took.

This place was strange.

A lot of it looked like any Southern California town of the early twenty-first century, of course. But there were a good many new high-rise buildings too, twenty or thirty storeys high. Sean didn't remember high rises being so common out here. And they were buildings of an astonishing weirdness of design.

One had twin curving spikes on its roof, like gigantic horns. Another had a strip of mirrors a yard wide running down its front from top to bottom. A number of buildings had large, eye-shaped glass ovals above their entrances, and some had additional eyes higher up on the facade. Decorations? Or mysterious electronic devices? And the architects had apparently hated straight lines. All of the buildings had odd wriggling edges, sinuous and fluted and swirly. Sean couldn't look for long at any one of them without feeling that he was being pulled around the corner into some other dimension.

The newer cars in the streets had the same twisting, looping lines. They were low and long and somehow sinister-looking, with single bands of grillwork across their fronts where headlights should be, and peculiar arching ornaments – or antennae? – rising in startling curves from their roofs. Some were carrying horn-like spikes similar to those on the building down the street. So a whole new kind of design would come into fashion in the years just ahead. He couldn't say that he admired it much.

The strangest thing of all was that there was no one in the streets.

No one. No one at all. He was all alone. He might have been the only human being in the whole world. He stood in the middle of the wide street under a warm midday sun, looking this way and that. No people in sight. No cars moved, no horns honked. Not a sound anywhere.

What had happened here?

Where was everybody?

This was starting to feel creepy. Frowning, Sean began to walk towards the building with the mirrored facade. Looking up, he saw his own image, broken and refracted a dozen times over. The entrance to the building was a wall of glass three times as tall as he was, decorated only by a jutting blue sphere that he assumed was some kind of doorknob. Hesitantly he put his hand to it.

The moment he touched it, music filled the air.

It came from everywhere at once, a hundred electronic brass bands blaring a hundred marching tunes. He whirled around, astonished, and saw lights suddenly blazing in every building, dazzling fireworks exploding overhead – fireworks in *daytime!* – banners unfolding from gravity-rotor platforms that had come spinning out from invisible hiding places.

He stared in amazement, trying to read all the banners at once.

WELCOME, SEAN!
THE CITY OF GLENDORA GREETS THE MAN FROM TIME!
GREATER LOS ANGELES CHAMBER OF COMMERCE SAYS
HELLO, SEAN!
THE YEAR 2025 IS GLAD TO SEE YOU!
SAN BERNARDINO COUNTY, CALIFORNIA'S GREATEST,
IS ALL YOURS!
HERE'S TO YOU — THE FIRST AND FINEST
TIME TRAVELLER

He glanced up the wide street and saw the marchers advancing towards him now. What seemed like thousands of people, stretching off into the distance as far as he could see.

Of course. This was probably the biggest day in the history of this little town. And they had had nine years to prepare for it.

'Good God,' Sean murmured. 'I'm famous! And here comes the parade!'

15

Eric $+ 5 \times 10^7$ minutes

It was hot and steamy here, a dense, lush, tropical heat. Just drawing a breath was hard work. The humid air wrapped itself around him like a heavy cloak. The thick sweet perfume of a billion flowers lay upon the air. The sky had a curious greenish colour, beautiful in its way, but strange and oddly troubling.

This time, Eric thought, the spatial displacement must have moved him clear out to Hawaii, or one of the South Pacific isles.

But something didn't seem right. Tropical islands were always warm but never this hot. The temperature must be well over a hundred degrees here. *Well* over. He had sometimes experienced heat like this, or almost like this, on field trips out in the desert. But that had been dry heat, torrid yet bearable. This stuff was something else, like being in a steam room. Or worse. Not even the desert got this hot very often.

Where am I? he wondered.

He looked around. There was a wide beach in front of him, crowded with sunbathers. It didn't have the exotic look of a tropical beach – crystalline water and white powdery sand. It looked very much like a Californian beach. Turning, he could see a town or small city a little way inland, and, behind the town, a steeply rising wall of rugged, heavily forested mountains.

It all seemed very familiar.

It definitely had the look of the California coast – up by Santa Barbara, say, where the mountains come down close to the shore. Though these mountains seemed a little closer to the shore than he remembered from his visit to Santa Barbara.

But what about this sweltering tropical heat? You almost never got temperatures like this along the Californian coast. And this stifling humidity? Never. Where were the cooling sea breezes? Puzzled, he walked up towards the promenade separating the beach from the town. Here the vegetation seemed wrong. The slim, graceful palm trees that were growing everywhere didn't look like the ones he had known all his life. They were more tropical species, most likely – coconut palms or royals palms or something else, something too tender to grow in California's mild but sometimes chilly climate. And these vines, these creepers, these odd ferns, these riotously blossoming shrubs with glistening leaves – no, no, Eric thought, none of this is California stuff. California is dry all summer long. These plants must come from some moist jungle.

He paused to catch his breath. Moving around was a real struggle in this greenhouse environment.

Where am I? he wondered again.

He had to be fifty million minutes in the future – a little more than ninety-five years. So this was the summer of the year 2111. If he was still alive in this year, he'd be 118 years old. Stretching his luck a little, maybe.

So he knew *when* he was. But *where – where?*

And suddenly he knew. This *greenhouse environment.* That was what he had called it a moment ago. He trembled with fear and shock as full understanding hit him. He was in California, all right. But a California that had been utterly transformed – in a world that had undergone what must have been a colossal calamity. . . .

'You savah, mister?' asked someone at his elbow.

A girl, aged about thirteen or fourteen. She was wearing only the tiniest of bathing suits and she had a small metallic pack strapped to her back. A flexible tube ran from the backpack to her mouth. A tall boy stood behind her. He had a similar backpack on.

'Savah?' Eric repeated. 'I don't understand.'

'Are you savah?' she said again. 'Are you all right? Are you okay?' She said 'okay' as if it was a word from a foreign language. 'You don't have your breather on.'

'No,' he said, 'I don't have one.'

'You lose it? You look bad mal, savvy? Tray mal.'

She was speaking a sort of French, he realized, French and English, mixed. He leaned on the railing of the promenade. She was telling him that he looked sick. And he felt sick.

'The air,' he said. 'So thick – so humid here, so hot—'

'Not the heat,' said the girl. 'It's the see-oh. It'll plonk you in a quick.'

See-oh. C-O, he thought. CO_2. Carbon dioxide.

'Lend him your breather, Slowjoe,' the girl said impatiently, gesturing to her companion. 'Can't you see he's going to plonk?'

Eric was feeling dizzier and dizzier. Vaguely he was aware of the boy unstrapping the device from his back and handing it to him. The girl put the tube in his mouth and told him to breathe deeply. Almost at once his head began to clear. Oxygen? They were watching him worriedly. Nice

71

kids, he thought. Lucky for me.

'Savah?' she asked. 'Better now?'

'Much,' he said.

'Bien. Go on. Put it on your back.'

'But I can't let him give me his breather.'

'He'll go and get another one. Five minutes without won't mort him. We're used to this stuff, you know.'

Eric nodded. *This stuff.* So it had really happened, he thought. The greenhouse effect that the environmental scientists had worried about all those years. The build-up of carbon dioxide in the atmosphere through the centuries of industrial development, until a thick mantle of heat-retaining gas surrounded the earth and temperatures everywhere started to climb. And the polar ice caps melted, and the seas rose, and the air turned into chemical soup, and the temperate lands turned into steaming tropics, and God only knew what had become of the places that had been tropical before.

Now Sean understood why the mountains here seemed closer to the shore than he thought they ought to be. The mountains hadn't moved. The rising seas had come up on to the land. If sea levels have risen twenty-five or fifty feet, he thought, what has become of Santa Monica? Of New York? The hills of San Francisco must be islands now.

'What's the name of this town?' he asked the girl.

'Santa Barbara,' she said.

'Santa Barbara, California.'

'No, Santa Barbara on the moon.' And she laughed. 'Where do you think you are?'

'I thought it might be Santa Barbara,' he said. 'But everything's so different from what I . . .' he paused.

'Go on,' she said. 'Different from what you remember, right?'

'You know who I am?'

'You're a voyager, yes? A time traveller? You come from

72

the cool years, right?'

'The cool years, yes. From the year 2016 as a matter of fact.'

The girl smiled. She didn't seem notably startled by what he had just said. Time travellers must be commonplace items by now, he thought. People dropping in from the past all the time. 'I knew it toot sweet, right away. You talk like the vieux-time people. You must have been one of the first, no?'

'The first,' he said. 'The very first.'

'No blague!' she said admiringly. 'Imagine that!' But she still didn't sound enormously impressed. 'Well, enjoy yourself here. If you can. Don't forget to use your breather. You'll plonk real fast without it, you know. *Real* fast.'

16

Sean $- 5 \times 10^7$ minutes

'Well, here comes the parade at last,' said the short red-faced man just to Sean's left.

What, again? The parade was over. Was time backing up on him? Had the pendulum slipped a cog? Yes, he could hear the sounds of parade music all over again. Had he somehow been taken a shunt within a shunt, going back to the start of his stay in 2025 to live through an experience he had already had?

'Yes, sir, that's what I call a parade!' the red-faced man said.

Sean stared. It was a parade, all right, but not the one he had just been in. He could see the prancing drum major now, far down the street. The half-built, dinky-looking, antiquated street. And he could hear the music. Not electronic sounds, no, but an old-fashioned brass band making a joyous blaring uproar. A real bass drum sending out vast booming sounds.

This wasn't Glendora in the year 2025. And this wasn't

any parade in honour of Sean Gabrielson, the visitor from out of time. Not at all.

He was in a small town, but it was a much older one. There weren't any futuristic high-rise buildings with horns and eyes on them. There weren't any high rises at all, just little wooden or stucco one- and two-storey buildings with scrawny young palm trees standing in front of them. And the sign on the street corner – an old-fashioned sign, white letters on blue metal, no fluorescence – said that this was Wilshire Boulevard.

So the name of this small town was Los Angeles. There wasn't much to it, back here in this year that he realized now must be 1921. The hills to the north were bare. The lofty embankments of the freeways were nowhere to be seen. The street was paved, but it looked like a country lane, hardly fit for heavy traffic. Everything had a raw, new look to it.

Boom! boom! boom!

The red-faced man pointed and waved, clapping his hands in glee. He didn't seem to be bothered by the fact that Sean has just materialized out of nowhere beside him. Or that Sean was dressed in the strange clothes of another era, an era yet unborn. Well, this was Hollywood, after all. The man probably thought that Sean was in costume for some science-fiction movie and had just stepped out of the studio to see the parade.

It was a fine spring day. The air was fresh and clean. They haven't even invented smog yet, Sean thought in astonishment.

It all looked so peculiar here. And yet not as peculiar as he had expected. In a way he was surprised to see that 1921 was in actual living colour, not in black and white, and that the people moved at a normal pace, not in some jerky frenzy. He had seen ancient films and he realized that he really had imagined that everything in reality would look the way it did in those films – quaint, musty, unreal. Well, it was quaint and musty, yes. But not unreal.

Sean turned to the red-faced man. He was wearing a stiff, uncomfortable dark suit, a necktie, a vest. On a warm spring day like this. But everybody else nearby along the parade route was dressed the same way. So formal, so elaborate. Neckties! Vests! The women all had hats on. And gloves. They were the ones who seemed to be in film costumes, not him. But this was no film for these people. This was the real world of 1921, and in that world, this was how people dressed.

'What's the parade all about?' Sean asked.

The man frowned at him. 'Why, in honour of the President.'

'The President,' Sean said. 'Ah – is the President here?'

'The President's in Washington, getting sworn in. Don't you know that? But even if we're three thousand miles away, we can celebrate. Yes, sirree! We're having a parade to honour the new President. Can't you see the banners?'

Sean turned and looked. The main float was passing by right now. Real orange trees, laden with fruit, on top of a horse-drawn platform. And banners, painted on canvas:

WARREN GAMALIEL HARDING, PRESIDENT OF THE
UNITED STATES
CALVIN COOLIDGE, VICE PRESIDENT
INAUGURATION DAY 4 MARCH 1921

'Three cheers for President Harding!' the red-faced man shouted, waving his hat in the air. 'He's my man! America first! No more wars! Back to normal! Harding! Harding! Harding!' He nudged Sean in the ribs. 'What's the matter, are you a Democrat? Let's hear you cheer!'

Sean nodded. Why not?

When in Rome, do as the Romans do. When in 1921,

give a cheer for the new President, if that's what everybody all around you is doing.

'Harding!' he yelled. 'Harding! Harding! Three cheers for President Harding!'

17

Eric $- 5 \times 10^8$ minutes

Eric felt a rush of cool sweet air, almost dizzying. After the
dank, moist, thick soup that was the air of Santa Barbara in
the year 2111, this was like fresh new wine. He was in a
forest of towering redwood trees, so tall their tops were
lost in the mist high overhead. He reached up to take the
breathing device from his mouth.

But the breather was gone. Of course. It was impossible
to carry any physical object from one shunt to the next
except the things he had had with him when the trip
began. The laws of conservation of energy were very strict
about that. Whatever gear he had set out with from Time
Zero would stay with him throughout the journey, but
nothing that he picked up along the way could be
transported. There wasn't any possibility of returning
from the past with a lost painting of Leonardo da Vinci
under your arm, or coming back from the future with
some fantastic device that would change the whole world.

Well, he didn't need any gadgets to help him breathe

here. This air was the purest he had ever known. He couldn't even imagine how air could be cleaner or fresher than this.

He checked his instruments. Longitude 121 degrees W. He was still in California, then. Latitude a little more than 36 degrees N. That would put him a bit north of the midway line between Los Angeles and San Francisco – somewhere around Monterey, Eric guessed. A pretty hefty spatial displacement this time. But he was 500 million minutes in the past, now. That was 951.3 years. By his best calculation this was a mild, misty January morning in the year AD 1065.

The forest was beautiful. He had never seen a lovelier place than this.

The mighty chocolate-red redwood trunks were like the columns of a vast cathedral. Far above him, nearly four hundred feet up, the treetops met in a roof of foliage. A pearly twilight glow was all that broke through to brighten the forest floor. The stillness was fantastic. He could hear no sound except the gentle patter of the droplets of condensed fog that fell to the soft needle-carpeted floor, and the distant murmur of a brook. The fronds of huge glistening ferns were everywhere about him.

The year 1065! In Europe now, the man who would be called William the Conqueror was laying his plans for the invasion of England. The Crusades would soon be beginning. There were great native American empires in Mexico and Peru. And at this moment, who knew what was happening at the palaces of China, Africa, or the Baghdad of the Arabian Nights?

He felt a moment of something very like regret at finding himself in this place.

If the spatial displacement had been greater, this shunt might have dropped him down in the hectic midst of history – in Rome, say, or Constantinople, or Venice, or perhaps one of the stone cities of Mayas. But here – here in this peaceful redwood forest on the California coast – Eric was as alone as though this was the dawn of time. There was no trace here of whatever sparse and scattered Indian population California had at this time. All was silence. All was peace.

That pang of regret vanished as suddenly as it had come. To be allowed to see such beauty as this was a privilege beyond measure. How could he yearn for some other place?

Quietly, struck by wonder, Eric wandered through the stupendous groves of trees. He thought of the California he had left behind, the roar of the freeways, the droning of the planes overhead, the immense sprawl of the cities. They had saved a few little redwood forests, sure, somewhere far up north of San Francisco. Like museum exhibits. But everywhere else the hand of man had left its mark.

And this was how it all had looked before we came, he thought.

Here, in this awesome solitude, in this place where perhaps no human being had walked before, he felt himself suddenly swept by an emotion that was completely new to him. He wanted to drop down to his knees and give thanks – to whom, to what, he wasn't really certain – for the beauty he beheld. He had never done such a thing before. Even now he hesitated, embarrassed, self-conscious.

Go on, he thought. Nobody's watching. And even if somebody was, so what?

But it was too late. The moment had passed. It would be forced, artificial, unreal, for him to do it now. Instead he stood quietly, resting his hand lightly on the giant trunk of a tree by the edge of the little stream.

He felt the strength of it, the immensity. This tree, he

thought, had made a great voyage through time, of a sort, itself. It must have been living when Jesus was born. Or even earlier. And on and on through the centuries to this year of 1065, and on beyond. Probably it would still be here in 1865 or 1875 or 1885 or whenever it was that men would come along with their saws and hatchets to cut it down. It might have lived on into the twenty-first century, the twenty-second, even the thirty-second, if it had been left to finish its long journey undisturbed.

After a while he walked on. He had no regret now that the shunt had brought him here, instead of to some busy capital of the medieval world. This moment out of time, this quiet interlude in the strange fantastic journey that the swinging pendulum had launched him on, was worth a thousand Constantinoples.

He smiled. And then he dropped to his knees after all, and bowed his head, and gave thanks and praise, not knowing to whom or to what. For this beauty, for this moment of peace: thanks and praise. Thanks and praise.

18

Sean + 5×10^8 minutes

'Alt! No podo pasari! Todos tempuus vorbudt aqui!'

'Are you speaking to me?' Sean asked the huge mechanical creature that loomed before him.

'Anglic!' the great gleaming robot cried. 'Du spikke Anglic! Yis u no?'

'Yis,' Sean said, bluffing for all he was worth. 'Ik spikke Anglic. Yis.'

The thing was at least nine feet high, and it was all eyes and mouth. Half a dozen huge, sparkling eyes ran around its upper end, some kind of band of sensors that flickered restlessly up and down the whole spectrum and probably beyond it into the infrared and the ultraviolet. And an ugly gaping slot of a mouth, big as the top of a rubbish bin, in its belly. The better to swallow you with, my little time traveller. Du spikke Anglic? Answer yis u no, or I'll gobble you up!

Sean looked around uneasily. He was standing on some rubbery catwalk suspended about twenty feet above what might have been a street. The street looked rubbery too, with purple pumpkin-shaped growths sprouting from it at intervals of eight or ten feet. To his right was what looked like a wall of ice, a smooth glacial face rising to an enormous height. He could see people moving around freely within the ice. So it wasn't ice and not a glacier, but a building of some sort. On the other side of him the street was lined with giant metallic needles the size of telephone poles. They were glowing pale purple and giving off soft twanging sounds.

So this is the year AD 2967, Sean thought. Well, it sure looks like the year AD 2967.

'Anglic,' the huge robot said. 'Du spikke Anglic.' Something was rumbling in its interior, making a cement-mixer sound. The eye-band turned a blazing yellow, then slowly subsided into orange and red. Small portholes on the robot's sides opened and swivelled. Projections like the feet of insects came poking out of them, waving and wriggling about.

It means to swallow me, Sean thought. As soon as it can figure out what I am. I'm going to be a tin can's afternoon snack.

He wondered what would happen to him if he turned and tried to make a run for it. Probably a bad idea. He imagined jets of gluey liquid squirting from those portholes and stunning him at fifty paces.

'Anglic,' said the robot again. 'You are a speaker of Anglic. Yes. Yes. Mode adjustment made. Comprendus? You are a tempuu and Anglic is your sprak. Comprendus? Comprendus? Rispondim! Do you comprendan?'

'You don't quite have it right yet,' Sean said. 'But keep trying.'

'No comprendus?'

'No comprendus, right.'

'Correction mode. Correction mode.' The robot began

83

sputtering and mumbling to itself. Cautiously Sean started to back away, moving very slowly. Maybe it won't notice that I'm leaving. The sounds from the metallic poles to his left grew higher in pitch. People were pointing at him through the glassy walls of the artificial glacier. 'You will cease departing,' the robot said. 'Correction has been made. We use your mode now. You are Anglic-speaking time traveller, unauthorized. You will us show your documentuus.'

'Documents,' Sean said. 'That's better Anglic. English, we call it. But I don't have any documents. I'm too early for that. I come from the year—'

'No documentuus! No documentuus!' The robot's eye-band flashed vivid scarlet. 'Illicitimu! Tempuu vorbudtu! No podo pasari!' It was getting really excited. The enormous frog-like mouth was opening and closing. Sean saw lights flashing inside, and gears moving about. It began to move towards him in a slow, ponderous way.

It *is* going to gobble me up, he thought. Because I'm an unregistered time traveller and I don't have the right passport. Or something.

He turned and started to run.

'No!' a voice cried behind him. 'Alt! No flikken! Is safe! Is okay! I to do, you will safe!'

A girl, a woman – he couldn't tell which, he couldn't begin to guess her age – emerged out of nowhere. She was very slender and taller than he was. She had glistening silver hair and silver eyes too, and her skin was bright red, the colour of a ripe apple. She looked strange, but she looked beautiful, too.

She might have been the most beautiful woman he had ever seen.

Darting swiftly around him, she ran right up to the giant robot and slapped the palm of her hand against its midsection. A panel opened at once. She reached in and

84

pressed a key. Instantly the robot's eye-band colour shifted towards blue. 'Podo pasari,' the robot muttered. 'Tempuu licitimu. Validimu. Propriu.' And it moved off, still muttering to itself.

The woman smiled. Her silver eyes dazzled him.

'You will forgive,' she said. 'My Anglic. Is not big good. But you will safe now.' Her voice was deep and rich and warm, with an odd little crack in it. It was like no voice he had ever heard, but very beautiful. Her hand reached towards his. 'They do not like tempuus, this year. Time travellers. Too many come, too much confuse. But I will protect. My people will. How is your name?'

'Sean,' he said. 'Sean Gabrielson. From the year 2016.'

'I bin Hepta-Noni-Acanta-Leela-Quintu-Quintu,' she said.

'Is all that your name?'

'I am to you Quintu-Leela,' she said, and laughed. Her laughter was magical. From the humming telephone poles came an answering sound, delicate and eerie. Her hand tightened on his. 'Come with me. You will safe with me. I will show the world.' Again the laugh. 'Everything. You and me, we bin amicuus. Friends, you say? Friends. We bin very warm friends. Comprendus?'

Sean nodded. He felt as though an electric current was passing from her hand into his. Perhaps it was. Quintu-Leela, he thought. The sound of her voice was marvellously strange and strangely marvellous. And those silver eyes. He imagined her name and his entwined within a heart, blazing a purple fire in the sky.

Love at first sight, that was what it was.

He had heard about such things but he had never really believed they happened. Especially to him. Love at first sight! Was that too crazy? Quintu-Leela and Sean. Sean and Quintu-Leela. God, she was beautiful! And fascinating! That voice! Those eyes!

85

Yes, I do believe I'm falling in love, he thought.

With a woman who lives in the time of my own great-great-great-great-great-great-great-granddaughter. Who for all I know could *be* my own great-great-great-great-great-great-great-granddaughter. The woman of my dreams, an incredible woman, a phenomenal woman, and any hour now, maybe any minute now, the displacement force is going to sweep me away from her forever.

19

Eric $+ 5 \times 10^9$ minutes

The tunnels went on and on, an endless maze, one smooth, shining onyx-walled corridor after another. Eric had no idea where he was or where he had been or where he was heading. All he knew was that he was somewhere below the surface of the earth, plodding through corridor after corridor after corridor, never once getting a glimpse of the sun, the sky, the stars. And never once seeing another human being.

He wondered how far underground he was.

He wondered whether any life, human or otherwise, still existed on earth's surface, here in the hundred-and-sixteenth century AD.

He wondered if he was still on earth at all.

This was his third day in the tunnels now. At least that was what the chronometer said. But his mind and body were both hopelessly confused down here, where there was no day, no night, only the unending onyx walls lit by some mysterious radiance deep within the stone. He felt almost no need for sleep. When he did, he simply slouched up against the tunnel wall and closed his eyes for half an hour or so. He ate just as sparsely. Now and then he remembered to consume one of the food tablets from his utility belt. Most of the time he was content to coast along on the slow-release nutrient additives that the Project Pendulum medics had pumped into his bloodstream a few hours before Time Zero.

It had been a fantastic experience at first, roaming this mystifying underground world of the far future. None of his previous shunts had shown him anything remotely as strange as this. But the fascination was beginning to wear thin for him.

He had arrived in a glow of dense emerald light. It was all around, engulfing everything, so that he could almost believe he was at the bottom of the sea. The light was so deep and so strong that it was impossible for him to make out any features of his surroundings whatsoever.

Then the light vanished as though a hood had been thrown over his head, and he found himself in a zone of the deepest blackness he had ever known. For a long while after that nothing happened. He stood in complete silence, mystified, uncertain.

'Hello?' he said. 'Anybody there?'

Nothing. No one. Silence.

He took a step. Another. Another. He was unable to see a thing. For all he knew, there was a pit a mile deep right in front of him. But he couldn't just stand here forever, waiting for things to happen. He went on, step by uneasy step.

There was a sweetness in the air, and something else, a touch of lemon, perhaps, or sage, or both at once. He wasn't surprised. Each era he had visited so far had had a distant and characteristic flavour. He hadn't expected that, that every time would smell different from all other times.

This is the smell of the hundred-and-sixteenth century, he thought. It was a likeable odour, but unreal and synthetic.

Perhaps they make their own air in the year AD 11529, he thought. He imagined giant air-making machines on the borders of every city, releasing flavours of every desired sort into the atmosphere. Maybe that was how they had coped with the build-up of carbon dioxide that had turned the whole world into a giant greenhouse in the twenty-second century. Just thinking about the time he had spent in that sweltering tropical world made him feel sweaty and weak. The air is a lot better here, he thought. Of course the greenhouse-effect problems were ancient history to the people of this era. Nine thousand years in the past, in fact.

That was before he realized that he wasn't breathing surface air at all. He was underground.

He put out his hand and touched smoothness to his left: highly polished stone. The moment he touched it, it lit up, and he saw that he was in a long cavern or corridor that stretched far in front of him, disappearing into dimness hundreds of yards away. The walls curved gently up to meet the rounded arch of the ceiling. He recognized the glossy brown stone as onyx, though it was astonishing to think of a corridor this size wholly lined with that rare and beautiful mineral. Synthetic onyx, maybe, he thought. This is the hundred-and-sixteenth century. They can do anything. There was pale light pulsing within the walls, an inexplicable inner radiance, cool and beautiful.

In awe and wonder he walked on. After a little while he saw figures moving slowly towards him and he halted, narrowing his eyes to peer into the distance. He felt curiously unafraid. This was too much like a dream to seem real. And in any case he was confident that the beings of this future age would be too civilized to offer him any harm.

They came closer, within the range of his vision now. They weren't human.

They were cone-shaped beings eight or nine feet high, with brilliant orange eyes the size of platters and rubbery blue bodies. Clusters of scarlet tentacles dangled like nests of snakes from their shoulders. They walked in an odd gliding, lurching way on suction pads that made a peculiar slurping sound as they clamped down and pulled free again.

No way could evolution have transformed the human race into creatures like this, Eric thought. Not in nine thousand five hundred years, not ever. These had to be aliens of some sort. There were half a dozen of them moving in a solemn procession along the opposite side of the corridor wall. He stared up at them. They were gigantic looming presences, massive, menacing.

He felt the first pricklings of fear. Being a traveller out of time gave him no invulnerability, only the illusion of it. This might be dream-like but it was no dream, and those creatures were twice his size. Would they try to harm him? He stood poised on the balls of his feet, ready to bolt and dart past them at the first hostile sign.

But they paid no attention to him. Like a procession of mourners they shuffled towards him and past him, not giving him so much as a glance. They seemed completely preoccupied with their own ponderous thoughts.

Eric stared at them in amazement.

Was he so insignificant to them? No more important than a squirrel by the side of the road? Had he come nine thousand five hundred years to be totally ignored?

Suddenly crazy fury blossomed in him.

'Hey!' he called. 'Wait! Aren't you even going to stop and ask the time of day? Don't you wonder what I am?'

They kept on going without looking back at him.

Eric shook his head. Anger gave way to bewilderment.

'I sure as hell wonder what you are,' he muttered lamely.

The huge creatures continued to shuffle on down the corridor. They dwindled in the dimness until he could barely see them. And then, at a place where the corridor seemed to curve slightly to the right, all at once they disappeared, vanishing like soap bubbles in the air.

Frowning, Eric struggled to understand. Had they found some passage?

Maybe they had never been there at all. Maybe they had simply been hallucinations. Maybe this *was* all a dream.

He ran back after them.

When he came to the place where the giant creatures had disappeared he could find no trace of doorways or side passages. The walls of the corridor were as smooth and unbroken here as they had been from the start.

He shrugged, turned back in the other direction, and marched on.

After what seemed like hours more of plodding along the same empty hallway Eric reached a place where the corridor swelled and split into nine apparently identical tunnels. At random he entered the third tunnel from the left. It too seemed to be empty. But then once again he saw a procession of strange beings coming towards him.

These looked like giant purple starfish with rough pebbly skins. Each had a globe of brilliant white flames glowing at the centre of its body and fifteen or twenty rigid tentacles radiating stiffly outwards. The way that they moved was to roll along with weird grace on the tips of their tentacles, like acrobats turning cartwheels.

'Excuse, me,' Eric said at once. 'I'm Eric Gabrielson. I'm a time traveller from the twenty-first century AD and—'

No use. They weren't any more interested in him than the suction-footed giants had been.

He watched in dismay as the starfish went rolling onwards and beyond. When they were a hundred yards or so past him they all abruptly turned to the left and pressed themselves against the corridor wall, which emitted a painful blue glow the moment they touched it. Eric covered his eyes.

When it seemed safe to open them again, there was no sign of the starfish creatures. Had they stepped right through the corridor wall?

Puzzled, he backtracked and studied the wall. It looked no different from any other section of the wall. After a moment's hesitation he touched it with the palm of his hand. Nothing happened. No blinding blue glow, nothing.

He went on.

He slept a little while. He nibbled a couple of food tablets.

He came to another place where the tunnel forked once more, branching into seventeen passages this time. He chose the rightmost branch. The tunnel was the same as before – smooth and glossy, and bright with that inexplicable inner radiance.

More beings appeared, seemingly floating in the air. They were elongated transparent creatures filled with churning misty organs. They looked like the sort of things you might see under the microscope in a drop of water, blown up to giant size – huge protozoa, a tribe of colossal paramecia.

'Hello?' he ventured. 'Does anybody here know what a human being is! Or was?'

The giant protozoa didn't seem to be interested in conversation, either.

Nor were the next creatures that he met, nor the next, nor the ones after that. Branch after branch, tunnel after tunnel, and it was always the same: silence, gleaming walls stretching far out before him, occasional bands of grotesque beings traversing the infinite corridors bound on unimaginable mysterious migrations. Sometimes they seemed to disappear into the corridor walls, as the starfish had done. Sometimes they seemed to emerge from the walls just as mysteriously.

Eric might just as well have been invisible.

What had begun as an eerily fascinating experience was becoming maddening and frustrating. He found himself wondering how long it was going to be before the displacement force seized him and carried him out of here to his next shunt, ninety-five thousand years deep in the past. At least the past was a place that he felt he understood.

Then, late on the third day, two beings that might almost have been human stepped suddenly out of the corridor wall no more than twenty feet in front of him.

Eric realized after the first startled moment that they weren't human at all. Their bodies were impossibly long and narrow and their arms and legs were thin as whips, with elbows every twelve inches. Their hands had more than five fingers. Their lips were nothing but slits, their bare, waxy-looking skins were greenish-yellow, and their golden eyes seemed to be set on end, much longer than they were broad.

There might have been some evolutionary changes in the human race since his own time, but a mere ninety-five centuries could never have produced a transformation like this. They had to be some sort of aliens.

Strange as they were, they were humanoid, at any rate. Not giant paramecia or walking starfish or great shambling blue and orange monsters. And, unlike all the others, they hadn't simply walked past him without a glance and kept on going. They had actually stopped and were studying him with some interest. That gave him hope.

'Please,' he said. 'I'm lost. I don't have any idea where I am. Won't you help me?'

The two eerie humanoids exchanged a quick glance.

Another positive sign. It was the first reaction he had managed to get from any of the beings he had encountered in these corridors. But they remained silent.

'Talk to me,' he said. 'Somehow. There's got to be a way that you can communicate with me. I know there is.'

For a moment more they remained motionless. Then one of them made a gesture with its many fingers. In Eric's own time that gesture meant come closer. He had no notion what it might mean here. He decided to risk it.

When he was just a few paces from them they reached their long ropey arms towards him and touched their soft cool fingers to his. It was like touching an electric socket. A sudden tingling shock burst through him.

'No, wait—'

He tried to pull back, but he was unable to break the contact.

And then, amazingly, he felt intelligible words taking form in his mind.

There is no reason for you to fear us. Why would we want to harm you?

'I didn't know what was happening to me. Or what to expect. I – I –' He took a deep breath. 'I'm Eric Gabrielson. I come from the twenty-first century. There's been this experiment, you see, in time displacement, and—'

We know that. We are the anterstrin thelerimane.

They said it as though that explained everything.

'Oh,' he said. 'And this is earth, isn't it? In the year AD 11529?'

This is earth, yes. You are in the quarantine section.

'Quarantine?'

All new arrivals are placed in quarantine until their clearances come through. It is the law. Visitors from time must undergo clearance just as visitors from space do. Once you are cleared you will be permitted to visit Upper Earth.

'I see,' Eric said. 'And how long does it take to get a clearance?'

In some cases, no more than ten or twenty days. In others, perhaps fifty to a hundred years, or even longer. Centuries, sometimes.

Eric thought of the displacement force, gathering its irresistible momentum now, almost ready perhaps to sweep him away from this place.

'Can't it ever be done faster?' he asked.

There is much that must be determined before strangers can be released into Upper Earth. We ourselves have been here sixteen years, and our case is by no means settled. You may have to wait just as long.

'But I can't,' Eric protested. 'I'm shunting in time on pendulum swings. Do you understand what I'm saying? The next swing could carry me away in an hour or a minute, or a day. And then I'd never get to see what earth is like in this era.'

Oh, no, said the quiet mental voice of the anterstrin thelerimane. *You will not be suddenly carried away, we assure you. The rules are never broken. No one leaves quarantine until the galithismon permits it. You will stay here until your clearance comes. We promise you that. Even if you must remain in the quarantine tunnels for five hundred years.*

20

Sean − 5×10^9 minutes

It was almost noon by the time Sean came to the eastern rim of the broad mesa that he had been crossing since dawn. He peered over the edge and what he beheld in the dark valley below made him gasp with wonder.

Bison. Thousands of them, maybe millions, great shaggy brown beasts with their heavy heads down close to the ground. They were ripping fiercely at the thick lush grass of the valley as if trying to turn the place into a barren desert in a single day. The vast herd filled the valley as far as Sean could see. The cold, biting wind out of the east carried their odour to him, rank and musky and sharp.

At last. After three days of solitary wandering in this cool wet land that was supposed to be Arizona, seeing nothing bigger than a ground squirrel and feeling tension rising within him as silent emptiness gave way only to more emptiness, he was staring at more animals than he had ever seen in one place in his life. Giant animals. What he saw out there was probably one of the last of the great big-game herds that had survived from the Ice Age and still roamed the southwest here in the paleolithic past.

'Hey!' he called. 'Hey, all you bison! You're extinct, do you know that? You hear what I'm telling you? Lie down and roll over! You're extinct.'

Sean didn't expect the bison to pay any attention to him, and they didn't. They went right on grazing, tearing out enormous clumps of grass, shaking their huge heads almost angrily from side to side as they fed. He had simply needed to hear the sound of his own voice again.

The three days that he had spent trekking through this forlorn world of 5×10^9 minutes ago had been the loneliest days he had ever known. Especially after the shunt that had preceded this one. Lovely Quintu-Leela, his woman with silver eyes. How he missed her now! What pain that had been, seeing her waver and vanish before him as the displacement force pulled him onwards in time! She was like something half-remembered from a vivid dream, now. She was up there in the future, in bewildering, incomprehensible AD 2967. And he was back here, five billion minutes in his own past.

Five billion minutes! That was some 9,513 years. This was the world of 7500 BC, more or less. These bison belonged here. He was the intruder.

Everything was different here, everything was unfamiliar. The air, when it didn't reek of bison fur, had an odd crisp iron quality, a metallic harshness that Sean knew was simply its purity. He had never breathed truly fresh air before. The sky looked bigger and bluer, the horizon further away than it ought to be. The light was more intense. The water that flowed in the many streams which crossed these plains seemed to have a strange electric tingle to it because it was so clean.

This was a world without automobiles, without aeroplanes, without chemical factories, without anything that belched fumes into the air. Strange huge animals roamed freely, and human beings scarcely existed. Over on the other side of the world in the Near East and maybe China, the first little towns were being founded, but even there the world must still be unspoiled. It was almost impossible to comprehend how far he was from his own time. The pyramids of Egypt would not be built for another five thousand years.

And yet Sean knew he had only begun his voyage across the eons. By the time he reached the outer limits of the pendulum swing, this era would seem like the day before yesterday to him.

He looked out into the sea of bison before him.

Now he noticed other animals down there, too, moving on the edges of the great bison herd. To his left he saw a pack of large, long-legged wolf-like creatures with broad, heavy-looking heads and dense blue-black fur. They looked frightening, but there was something curiously unferocious about their movements: they were sniffing and snuffing around like scavengers hoping to find an easy meal, and even when a lost bison calf wandered past them they made no move to attack.

Farther to the left were three peculiar-looking, massive creatures squatting down on their haunches in front of a slender pine tree. Even squatting like that, they were taller than the tree. They were methodically pulling it apart, stripping the bark from its branches and cramming it into their mouths. Sean remembered seeing pictures of them on the orientation tape for this period: giant ground sloths. Deeper in the distance, so far across the valley that he could barely make them out, were mastodons. Their elephant-like forms were unmistakable. He saw some things that might have been camels out there, too. And closer at hand was a pair of heavy-looking creatures that seemed midway between an elephant and a pig in shape.

Giant tapirs, he supposed.

The experts had thought these creatures of the late Ice Age might be just about extinct, here in the Arizona of 7500 BC. But there was some uncertainty about the date of the great extinction and they had asked Sean to keep an eye out for them as he passed through this level of the shunt. And there they were. Beginning their decline, maybe, but far from extinct.

Mastodons! Bison! Giant ground sloths! What a fantastic sight!

As Sean stared out towards the far reaches of the valley, a sudden flash of activity closer at hand caught his attention. He looked down and to his left. The bison calf had strayed just a little too far. From a dense clump of bushes at the base of the mesa came now a quick and savage killer, long and low-slung, with a compact, powerful tiger-like body and two astounding, gleaming fangs almost a foot in length.

The calf never had a chance.

Swiftly the sabre-tooth pounced, rising from the ground with a fierce thrust of its strong back and loins and clamping its heavy forearms against the bison's shaggy hump. In the same instant those two great daggers rose and sank deep into the flesh of the bison. The calf shivered under the assault and sank to its knees, and then tumbled over, pushing desperately at the sabre-tooth with its hooves as though trying to shoo away any annoying fly.

It was all over in moments. Sombrely Sean watched the killer-cat feed, and then the wolves came forth, snarling with sudden fury, demanding their share. The sabre-tooth glared at them coldly as if ready to take on the whole pack. Then it wriggled its heavy neck in something remarkably like a shrug, and slowly moved off. It had eaten its fill, and now it was abandoning its prey to the hungry wolves. They were scavengers after all, terrifying though they might look.

Eventually the wolves, too, vanished into the thickets, leaving the bloody carcass for smaller beasts to devour.

Sean now warily began to make his way down the mesa's steeply sloping eastern face. He wanted a closer look at all these animals. Now that the most dangerous predator down there had had its lunch, the risks he faced were probably not great. And in any case he had an anaesthetic dart gun strapped in the utility belt around his waist, and a laser, too. The dart gun ought to be able to take care of most problems. He wasn't supposed to use the laser as a weapon except in the most desperate of circumstances. If he went around killing things with his laser in the remote past, he might be making significant changes in the fabric of time by removing this creature or that which hadn't originally been destined to die at the hands of a man from the far future. But his surviving the mission was important, too. He had to calculate the trade-offs before going for the weapon.

The soil was damp and soggy from the rain that had drenched these plains, and him, last night. As he descended he sank in almost an inch with every step, coming up with moist, sticky mud on his boots. Mud wasn't something he associated with Arizona. Or valleys rich with thick lush grass. The Arizona he knew was a place of parched wastelands, dry brittle soil, twisted thorny scrub vegetation. But his instrument reading showed that he was somewhere just to the north of the place where Phoenix would be in another nine thousand-odd years.

He had started out from Los Angeles, up there at Time Zero in AD 2016. Not only had the shunt displaced him in time, though, it had also moved him some four hundred miles in space. No surprise there. The pre-shunt calculations had predicted that. The longer the time-shunt, the farther the spatial displacement.

This was Arizona, all right. But it was prehistoric Arizona at the tail end of the Pleistocene Ice Age. The great chill that had brought so much moisture to this part of the continent had already begun to retreat; the lakes and meadows were starting to dry out, and the big game animals were becoming sparse. During his increasingly depressing three-day trek through the utter silence of this land he had begun to fear that they were already extinct. Now Sean knew that that was not so.

Slipping and sliding and stumbling, he made his way down the last twenty feet to the valley floor and found himself about a hundred yards from the nearest bison.

This close, he realized that they had little in common with the bison he had seen in zoos except the shagginess of their hides. These animals were gigantic, each one as big as a truck. They were colossal. They were immense. Their horns, instead of curving back to lose themselves in the heavy fur, jutted out three feet or more on each side. And the sound they made as they grazed was a mighty throbbing growl like the sound a fire makes as it roars through a dry forest.

He edged sideways, keeping his back to the mesa wall. A few of the bison closest to him eyed him without curiosity for a moment, but most did not even bother looking up. Why should they? They had no reason to fear him. They might never have seen a human being before. The whole human population of North America at this time was probably no more than twenty or thirty thousand widely scattered nomads. And to these bison he must seem utterly harmless, a flimsy little two-legged thing with no teeth or muscles worth worrying about and no claws at all.

Seeing that the bison were ignoring him, Sean moved out a little boldly into the valley. The hugeness of the animals filled him with awe. They were like mountains. Even the calves seemed immense. He had all the more respect now for the strength of that sabre-tooth.

He saw other animals now, smaller ones, animals he could not name. They were almost familiar – something that could almost have been a badger, and waddling birds that were somewhat like turkeys, and little scrambling rodents rather like guinea pigs. But they were all somehow different from their modern counterparts.

He wished he knew more about prehistoric zoology. This was an amazing place. Evidently this valley was a rich and fertile location that was particularly attractive to beasts great and small from all over central Arizona. What an amazing privilege it was to be allowed to see this congregation of great creatures!

Then he realized that he was not the only person here.

Shouts came from a fold in the valley floor a few hundred yards away. Glancing up in surprise, Sean was startled to see eight or ten tall, slender men in loincloths pelting one of the bison calves with rocks to drive it into a small box canyon. They were armed with spears tipped with tapering stone points, and as they pursued the angry, frightened calf they jabbed at it again and again, barely penetrating its thick furry hide. Killing it was going to be a difficult job.

Sean had been so concerned with the animals that he hadn't heard the hunters approach. Now, struck with wonder and amazement, he stepped back behind a tree to watch them in action. They were long-limbed, graceful men. They seemed almost to be floating as they ran along behind the calf. Though they had dark skins of a deep coppery hue, they looked very little like the Indians of his own time. Their heads were narrow and tapering, their shoulders sloped, their features were small, almost delicate. The chilly air seemed to bother them not at all, practically naked though they were.

He leaned forward, peering intently, fascinated by the

sight of these prehistoric hunters at their task.

Then he felt a sudden stiff jab between his shoulder blades.

He whirled. And found himself looking at another of the hunters, who had come up silently behind him. His eyes were dark and shining, almost glowing with a light of their own. They were fixed on Sean in absolute concentration. The hunter grasped a spear lightly in his left hand, balancing it easily by the middle of its shaft.

He must have used the wooden end of the spear to poke Sean in the back. But now he had swung it around the other way. Sean stared. The long, sharp, elegantly carved stone point of the spear came into close focus just in front of him. It was aimed at the centre of his chest, hovering just a couple of inches over his heart.

21

Eric − 5 × 10^{10} minutes

The rules are never broken. That was the last thing that he remembered the anterstin thelerimane saying, back in the tunnels that ran beneath the world of AD 11529. Those two spooky humanoids with the long whip-like limbs had seemed to be telling him that he was going to dwell in the tunnels forever. *No one leaves quarantine until the galithismon permits it. You will stay here until your clearance comes, we promise you that. Even if you must remain in the quarantine tunnels for five hundred years.*

And then he felt the familiar swooping, dizzying sensation that let him know he was making a shunt, and the anterstin thelerimane disappeared. The weird glistening tunnel with the onyx wall disappeared. The whole world of AD 11529 disappeared.

So much for the quarantine powers of the galithismon, Eric thought. Whoever or whatever the galithismon might be, it had been unable to withstand the power of the great pendulum that was carrying Eric back and forth across time.

What now? he wondered.

He found himself on an icy windswept plain, bleak and desolate. Leafless trees with dark crooked trunks rose here and there above the snowfields. The air was harsh and sharp, with howling gusts cutting deep. He touched his utility belt to give himself a little protection against the cold.

This was the minus-fifty-billion-minute level. Fifty billion minutes! He was 95,129 years into the past now – the Pleistocene period, the last Ice Age, the Fourth Glacial. Eric took his bearings. Latitude 41 degrees north. Longitude 6 degrees east. *East?* He was in Europe, then. Right in the middle of Spain. A whopping spatial displacement, clear across the whole United States and the Atlantic too. Halfway around the world and smack into the teeth of an Ice Age gale.

And there were tracks in the fresh snow in front of him.

Human tracks.

No question about it. The tracks had been made by someone with a wide foot, very wide. Probably a short person, because the prints were fairly close together.

But human, without a doubt. Because the feet that had left those tracks in the snow had been clad in sandals of some sort. The imprint was unmistakable: no sign of toes or claws, only the rounded front end of the sandal and the tapering heel.

Human? In Pleistocene Spain?

Neanderthals, Eric thought in sudden wonder. And he began to follow the trail.

It led up and over a hummock of rock that jutted from the snowfield, and down the other side through a region of loose and annoyingly deep snow that gave him much trouble, and then up the side of a steep hill. Climbing it was real work. For one bad moment he thought he had lost the trail altogether, but then he picked it up again, midway up the hill. Behind him, the winds grew wilder and snow began to fall. He scrambled upwards.

Then he saw a cave, a fire burning within.

He stared. Eight, ten people inside, close together by the campfire. Wearing shaggy fur robes, though some were bare to the waist. Short people, stocky and squat, with big heads and thick necks and barrel chests and broad, low-bridged noses. They weren't pretty, no. But they weren't apes, either. They were human beings. Different from us, but not by much. Cousins. Our Neanderthal cousins. Eric shivered, and not just from the cold.

One of them was singing, and the others were gathered around, nodding and clapping their hands in time. A slow, rhythmic chant, which suddenly speeded up, then slowed again, then speeded again; it was an intricate rhythm, constantly changing. Almost like a poem. Almost? It *was* a poem! Those complex rhythms, the solemnity of the chanter's voice, the rapt attention of the listeners. The *Iliad* of the Neanderthals, maybe, a tale of heroic battle deeds. Or the *Odyssey*, the story of a man who had gone to war across the sea and had had a hard time getting home. A tribal poet, telling the great old stories around the campfire. Stories that would fall into the deepest sort of oblivion when these rugged people of the Ice Age were swept away into extinction, thirty or forty thousand years from now.

Neanderthal poetry! The idea stunned and dazzled him.

He leaned forward as far as he dared, peering into the mouth of the cave, straining to hear the words, hoping with an impossible hope to understand the meaning.

Abruptly the chanting stopped. There was silence in the cave.

They knew he was there. How? He had crouched down behind a great rock partly blocking the entrance. But they were looking his way. Sniffing. Those big noses, those wide

106

nostrils. They could smell him. They were murmuring to each other. Suddenly these people seemed less like ancient cousins, more like hairy ogres or trolls.

The storm was lashing the plain now: wild winds, flailing the falling snow into thick white curtains. Eric backed away from the mouth of the cave. He heard a shout from within, then another and another. Desperately now he began to run down the hill, slipping and stumbling in the loosely packed snow.

And they were coming after him.

Don't try to run, he thought. Slide for it! Slide!

He dropped down flat and gave himself a shove. And went wildly tobogganing away, moving at an ever accelerating speed with his knees drawn up tight against his chest and his arms pulled in over them. A couple of times he fetched up against some upjutting snag of a tree, or some hunk of rock, and gave himself a nasty whack, but then he pushed on, down and down and down the hill.

After a time he looked back. The Neanderthals had stopped pursuing him. They were standing some distance above him on a snowy ridge, staring at him in what looked like open-mouthed astonishment.

They probably think I'm crazy, Eric thought. Crazy, skinny, peculiar-looking guy wearing a strange outfit, who can't find any better way to amuse himself than go sliding down a bumpy hill in the middle of a snowstorm. Obviously a low-IQ type, a real moron.

Or maybe not. Maybe they think I'm having a good time.

He stood up, waved, shouted to them.

'Come on!' he called. 'You try it, too! It's fun, guys! It's fun!'

He saw them muttering to each other. Maybe they were considering it. Maybe they were seriously thinking about taking up body-sledding, now that I've shown them the way.

I may have started something here, he thought. The Neanderthal Winter Olympics!

He brushed snow from his clothes and trudged on down the hillside, feeling a little creaky and battered. When he looked back next, the Neanderthal conference was still going on, and two of them were lying in the snow, trying to shove themselves downhill.

22

Sean + 5×10^{10} minutes

The point of the spear just barely grazed Sean's chest. The other man held it there. Sean froze, not even breathing. He looked down, eyes bulging, at the sharp stone tip against his breastbone. This is it, he thought. The end of Sean, nine thousand years ago in Arizona. The archaeologists will be really confused when they find the bones of a white man in the ancient strata here.

You have to do something, he told himself.

Go for the dart gun? Or even the laser? No. It took a little time to get the anaesthetic darts armed and primed. He didn't have that much time. As for the laser, he knew he was supposed to avoid using the weapon unless he had absolutely no other option. Besides, he suspected that the moment he made any movement towards his utility belt that spear would be sticking out of his back.

Do something. Anything.

He began to sing.

He had no idea what good it would do. He just opened his mouth and let melody come flowing out.

> Oh, say, can you see
> By the dawn's early light . . .

The hunter looked astounded. He stepped back, one pace, two, three, without taking his eyes off Sean.

Reprieve. Somehow.

> . . . what so proudly we hailed
> by the twilight's last gleaming . . .

The hunter spoke – a single stream of words punctuated by explosive little bursts of breath.

'Sorry,' Sean said. 'I don't speak Prehistoric Hopi, or whatever you're talking.' He managed a smile. It wasn't easy. It must have looked more like a tense grimace. Every culture understands smiling, he knew. Show your teeth. It's a sign of good will. 'You are a Hopi or something, right? An Indian, anyway. An early version. An ancestor. My name is Sean. I come here in peace from the year 2016. Do you want me to sing some more? "God rest ye merry gentlemen, let nothing you dismay—" '

The hunter spoke again, the same speech, faster this time. To Sean his words sounded blunt, cruel, and harsh.

Sean responded with another smile, a little on the edgy side. And came out with:

> California, here I come
> Right back where I started from . . .

It was hard to tell what the other was planning to do. The hunter's eyelids were fluttering now. His nostrils flared wide. He grasped his spear at both ends and pulled

110

it back tightly against his chest. He spoke once more, slowly and in a deeper voice. As if he were sinking into some sort of trance.

Keep on singing, Sean thought.

> I am the captain of the Pinafore
> And a right good captain too.
> De deedle deedle dee and deedle deedle dee
> With chimpanzees for my crew.

They weren't quite the right words, but he doubted that the hunter would know that. And at least the tune was there.

The other hunters were approaching now. Their faces were smeared with bison blood. One of them prodded Sean with the sharp end of his spear, pushing against the close-knit fabric of his jumpsuit. It was just the lightest of touches, but Sean shivered as he felt the keen tip of the stone point. He tried singing the 'Hallelujah' chorus. It didn't sound so good solo. They came in closer now, pinching and poking him. He switched to 'Silent Night' thinking it might calm them some. The first one, the one who seemed to have gone into a trance, made a low rumbling sound far back in his throat.

I'd like to get out of here, Sean thought. Somehow. Any way at all. Just let it be right now.

He smiled again, the widest smile he could manage. 'I know you can't understand a thing that I'm saying, but I'm saying it calmly and reasonably. I'm not here to cause any trouble. I'm simply a visitor. My name is Sean Gabrielson and I'm twenty-three years old and I have a degree in physics from Cal Tech, and I mean to keep right on speaking quietly and reasonably to you until you decide that I'm no threat. I'm also willing to sing anything you request. I can do some nice old rock numbers, I know a couple of hymns, I can do patriotic songs. And I can keep it up until the next shunt comes and gets me, if I have to. Just stand there and listen peacefully, okay?' He started in on 'Rock of Ages'. They all looked almost hypnotized now, their eyes wide and staring. They didn't know what to make of him.

'I can tell you all sorts of useful things, too. For example, I can advise you to start thinking about migrating north, because these animals here that you hunt are going to clear out of this territory in another few hundred years, once things start getting really warm and dry, and ...'

They were looking at him in what looked like awe. Maybe they're beginning to think I'm a god, he thought. Or maybe they just love the sound of my voice.

'You see, this is the late Pleistocene, but eventually this is going to be known as the state of Arizona, and I can prophesy that there's going to be a freeway right down the middle of this valley, running from Flagstaff down to Phoenix or Tucson ...'

They were down on their knees. Yes. Worshipping me, Sean thought. He grinned. They *do* think I'm a god. Unless they're just begging me to stop talking and start singing again.

Old Man River, that Old Man River ...

This is going to be fun, he told himself.

Then he felt the displacement force tugging at him.

Not now, he thought in annoyance. Not just when it's getting good? But there was nothing he could do about it. The force had pulled him away from Quintu-Leela and now it was yanking him away from his first good shot at being a god, or at least being a star singer. One moment he was staring at a bunch of awed prehistoric bison hunters, and the next he was floating in a globe of green light,

112

somewhere very far away.

So long, fellows. Onwards to – what?

This was serious future now, a truly major distance. He was 95,129 years down the line, an enormous jump. His last forward swing had taken him a mere 951 years ahead. Even that world, Quintu-Leela's world of AD 2967, was utterly unlike anything he knew or could understand. That was how vast the changes had been between his own time and Quintu-Leela's.

Now he was a hundred times as far from Time Zero – 95,129 years! The transformations in human life during such an immense span must have been incredible. It had taken only five thousand years to go from the first civilizations in Egypt and Mesopotamia to the age of travel through time and space. Now he had covered twenty times as many years. Did the human race even exist anymore? Or had it evolved into something unimaginably strange?

Where was he? What was this globe of green light? What was going to happen to him?

There were many questions, and no answers.

Then a deep, gentle voice said, 'Hey, it's good to see you again, Sean. Been a long time, boy.'

A very familiar voice. His grandfather's voice, rich and warm. Grandpa Gabrielson who lived in San Diego.

Sean blinked into the greenness. 'Is that you, Grandpa?'

'Who else, boy?'

Unmistakable, that voice. The voice of the wise, loving old man who had spent so many holiday weekends with them, who liked to tell all those stories of the first television sets, the first jet planes, the first trip to the moon, the first flights of the space shuttle. Grandpa Gabrielson had worked as an engineer for the Apollo space programme when he was a young man, and later he had been involved in the shuttle project. He had seen the whole modern world take shape in his lifetime.

But Grandpa Gabrielson had no business being here in the nine-hundred-and-thirty-second century. Grandpa Gabrielson had lived to a good old age, well past eighty. But he had died last year, just before Sean and Eric had been chosen for Project Pendulum.

'I'm here too, son. It really *has* been a long time!' It was his grandmother's voice. She had died when he was ten. And then his father was in the green globe with him, clapping him on the back and laughing, asking him if he was managing to keep up with the baseball scores while he was shunting around. And his mother, glowing with pride. And his mother's parents, Grandfather and Grandmother Weiss. He hardly knew them, because they lived in Belgium.

And Eric was there also.

It was Thanksgiving Day, and there was a huge turkey on the table, and mounds of cranberry sauce, and mountains of candied yams and turkey stuffing and everything else, and the whole family was there. His father was busy carving, as he always did. And he and Eric were side by side for the first time in 95,129 years.

Sean looked at his brother. He could feel the strange force, the brother-force, that had bound him to his twin all his life. The force which he had not felt since the moment they had gone their separate ways at Time Zero on the shunt platform.

'Are you really here?' he asked.

Eric grinned. 'What do you think? That I'm just some sleazy illusion?'

'But this can't be happening,' Sean said. 'Thanksgiving Day in the year 95,129? Grandpa and Grandma here? Mum and Dad? No. I'm in some kind of green globe and this is just some hallucination that who knows what kind of creatures are pulling out of the memories they find in my brain. Right? Right?'

114

Eric gave him a pitying look. 'You must have lost your mind. Or misplaced it at the very least. I'm as real as you are, and probably a lot hungrier. Shut up and pass the turkey, turkey!'

23

Eric + 5×10^{11} minutes

Scrambling down an icy hillside through a blinding snowstorm was bad enough. But every breath was agony. Breathing this fierce Fourth Ice Age atmosphere was like inhaling icicles. And to have a pack of angry Neanderthals coming after him, besides. . . .

Eric felt the shunt take him and sweep him mercifully into some far-off warmer place. He landed on all fours, gasping and coughing, and crouched there a moment until he had recovered. At last he looked up.

A Neanderthal face was looking back at him. Sloping forehead, rounded chin, broad nose, mouth like a jutting muzzle. Shrewd dark eyes studying him intently.

'Huh? Did I bring you along with me somehow?'

The Neanderthal knelt beside him and said something in an unknown language. His voice was deep and the way he spoke seemed oddly musical, though very strange. He didn't seem hostile. Behind him, Eric saw softly rounded green hills, a wide valley broken by a chain of lakes, and a forest in the distance.

There were prehistoric hominids wandering about wherever he looked.

He had landed in a group of ten or fifteen Neanderthals. Off to his left a hundred yards away were some slender little creatures that looked a bit like apes but walked confidently upright. Eric recognized them as australopithecines from the early Pleistocene, creatures that occupied a place somewhere midway on the evolutionary path that had led to *Homo sapiens*. And over there, that awesome monster of an ape, as massive as a grizzly bear? Wasn't that Gigantopithecus, from a million years BC? And those, in the middle distance? Sturdy-looking people who seemed almost human but for their strangely ape-like faces – could those be *Homo erectus,* the ancestors of mankind whose fossil remains had been found in Java and China?

And those –

And those –

And those –

Wherever he looked, some not-quite-human creatures could be seen in the valley. The whole history of evolution of humanity seemed to be here, all the extinct forms that he had studied in school and a good many that he was unable to identify at all.

What was this place? Unless he had lost count of the shunts, he was at the plus-500-billion-minute level now. 951,000 years in the future. What were all these creatures doing here, all wandering around at random like this?

'You have just arrived, I suppose?' a pleasant voice said behind him. Eric whirled. The speaker was a bearded man of about fifty, elegant and amiable-looking, wearing what looked like riding clothes of the late eighteenth or early nineteenth century. He might have been some English gentleman out for a stroll in the woods. 'Bathurst,' he said.

'Benjamin Bathurst. Former Minister Plenipotentiary of His Britannic Majesty George III to the court of Franz I, Emperor of Austria. Of course, I'm nothing very much any more.'

'Eric Gabrielson,' Eric said shakily. 'From Los Angeles, California, the – the United States.'

'Very pleased to make your acquaintance,' Bathurst said. 'Always charming to see another human face. There are forty of us now, I think. Of course, we're greatly outnumbered by the apes, but everyone's friendly enough. You're a million years in the future, you know. The United States, you say? Of America? The former Colonies? California was never one of the Colonies, as I recall. But I suppose—'

'We got it from Mexico,' Eric said. 'Somewhere around 1849. And yes, I know we're a million years in the future. Approximately. But you – George III . . .'

He was having trouble speaking clearly. An overdose of confusion was making his voice husky. The Neanderthal, muttering to himself, began to fondle Bathurst's intricately carved walking stick. The Englishman smiled and gently drew it away.

'What year are you from?' he asked Eric.

'2016 is when I set out from.'

'Ah. 2016. The fabulous future, indeed. Well, well, we will have much to talk about, then. No one else here comes from any year later than 1853, I believe. Most are much earlier. We have a Roman couple, do you know, and several Greeks, and an Egyptian or two. And some who speak no language any of us can fathom. They must be quite ancient. I myself was seized in 1809.'

'Seized?'

'Oh, yes, of course, boy! How do you think we all got here?'

Eric moistened his lips. 'I'm here as a result of an

experiment in travel through time carried out at the California Institute of Technology,' he said. 'But you—'

Bathurst shrugged. 'A victim of kidnapping. Forced transport. Seized unawares. The same fate that has befallen all the creatures here, both human and otherwise. Except you, it would seem, if you indeed have come voluntarily. The rest of us are captives. It is a very comfortable captivity, I must say, but it is captivity all the same. And it is imprisonment for life, I grieve to say. Yet it is a very comfortable imprisonment, for all that.'

Kidnapped from 1809? Romans? Greeks? Neanderthals? Australopithecines?

'But who – who—'

'Who is responsible for bringing us here, you mean to ask? Why, the demigods who inhabit this distant eon, boy! Our own remote descendants! Perhaps you'll meet them someday. I myself have seen them on three occasions thus far. Quite remarkable, you'll find. True demigods, as far beyond us as we are beyond these shaggy ape-like fellows here. We've been collected, do you see? All manner of historical specimens, and prehistorical specimens too, I dare say. It's a kind of zoological garden here. An exhibit, do you see, of the people of ages gone by, collected by mysterious magical means from every era of antiquity. I'm one of the items on display, boy, for the amusement and edification of our remote descendants. And now so are you, do you see? So are you.'

24

Sean − 5×10^{11} minutes

He was almost coming to believe that it was real. The tender, succulent turkey meat, the sweet, rich cranberry sauce, the hot steaming rolls – it was all so much like the family feasts of his boyhood that after a while he simply accepted it and let it engulf him like a warm bath. Mum, Dad, his grandparents, Eric—

But then it all turned misty and insubstantial. He had a final glimpse of the sphere of green light once again, and he thought he saw a row of faces behind the light, faces that might have been human and might have been something else. Then everything went black and the shunt took him and swept him away.

He was in heavy jungle terrain now. The air was thick and humid, the trees were tall and slender and set close together with their crowns meeting overhead to form a canopy. Here and there, through a break in the foliage, he saw pale sugarloaf-shaped mountains on the horizon.

This, he knew, was the world of 951,293 years before Time Zero.

And there was the biggest gorilla anyone had ever seen, standing twenty feet in front of him.

Actually he doubted that it was a gorilla. Perhaps it was more like an orangutan, with that deep chest and short neck. Or something midway between the two. But it was colossal. It was supporting itself on all fours, but he suspected that when it stood upright it would be close to nine feet tall.

It was watching him with a who-the-devil-are-*you*? look in its beady yellow eyes, and it was making a low growling sound, very ominous. Gorillas and orangutans, Sean told himself, eat fruit and vegetables. This guy doesn't look like a hunter to me. But he's big. Very big. And not friendly-looking. Absolutely not friendly. And I'm on his personal turf, and he doesn't like it.

'Listen,' Sean said. 'I don't want you to get annoyed about anything, okay? Just as I was telling those Indians a little while ago, it's not my plan to bother you in the slightest. I'm only a visitor here. I'm simply passing through, and I'm not going to be here very long, let me assure you of that.'

The giant ape appeared to frown. It seemed to consider what Sean was telling it.

It didn't seem to like what it had heard, though. It began to snort and growl. It raised itself to its full unbelievable height and pounded itself on its chest like King Kong in a bad mood. It made unmistakably angry sounds. Sean wondered if it was going to charge him. He wasn't sure. The ape didn't seem quite sure, either. For a long moment it rocked back and forth, growling, beating its chest, and glaring at the intruder.

Then it leaned forward on its knuckles and made a different sound, deep and ominous.

Yes, Sean thought. It *is* going to charge. It very definitely is going to charge.

And I'm going to die, back here in the umptieth century BC.

Or else I'll get shunted out of here in the nick of time and it's Eric who'll die when he shows up right in front of a crazed charging ape. It's just as bad either way.

Damn! Damn! *Damn!*

25

Eric − 5×10^{12} minutes

The shunts were coming too fast, too close together. Eric was drowning in a torrent of wonders. To be given a glimpse of Neanderthals in their own time, chanting by their own campfire, and then to be swept far on to a magical place where pithecanthropi and australopithecines and Romans and Greeks and nineteenth century English-men lived all jumbled together in some kind of far-future zoo, and to be pulled away from that much too soon, before he had even begun to learn the things he wanted to know.

And now this. Nine and a half million years in the past. Paradise for the sort of dreamer who once built fossil dinosaurs out of papier mâché. Not that there were any dinosaurs here, of course. Not in the Pliocene period, no. Dinosaurs were much earlier than that: this was mammal time, here. But, dinosaurs or no, he had been let loose in a garden of zoological wonders and he would gladly have spent a year here, or five years, or even ten. There was so much to see. Paleozoology wasn't even his field – he barely knew the names of half the creatures who were parading before his astounded eyes – and even so he would have given anything to be allowed to remain. Another month – another week....

But he knew that the irresistible force of the shunt would soon surround him and tear him free of this place and sweep him on.

That giant pig-like thing with the fantastic bristly face and the terrifying teeth, a creature bigger than any rhinoceros, snorting and snuffling in the underbrush –

That hairy elephant with the short trunk and the long thrusting jaw, and the second pair of tusks jutting down over the other ones –

That timid yellow animal with a camel's silly face and a gazelle's agile body, running in frantic herds across the plains –

That one that had a camel's body and a camel's head, but a neck like a giraffe's, reaching up easily to graze on treetops close to twenty-five feet high –

The deer with its horns on its nose, and the one with fangs like a tiger's, and the one whose head was all knobs and crests –

The giant ground sloth with the long, weird, drooping snout, almost like a little trunk –

The armadillo as big as a tank, angrily lashing its spiked tail against the ground –

Dream-animals. Nightmare-animals. They were everywhere on this wondrous plain – grazing, creeping, crawling, climbing, hunting, sleeping. He wanted to see every one, to commit them all to memory, to come home with mind-pictures of this Pliocene wonderland that would keep paleozoologists busy for decades. Unique discoveries, animals unknown to science. But already he felt the force tugging at him.

No, wait.... Another day, he begged. Half a day. Another three hours.

No chance. The equations were inexorable. Forces had to balance.

Now – now – onwards....

26

Sean $+ 5 \times 10^{12}$ minutes

He was five trillion minutes from home and the giant ape was no longer his immediate problem. Because the pendulum had swung and the iron fist of the displacement force had grabbed him and converted him into a shower of tachyons and sent him rocketing off towards the other end of time. So it was Eric who was destined to show up right in the path of the ape's charge, when they started down the homeward slope of the voyage.

I have to do something to warn him, Sean thought. But what?

He looked around. He was standing in a fragrant bower of blossoming plants that sprouted on shining crystalline stalks three feet high, plants that looked like nothing he had ever seen before. And a great blue world was shining overhead like a dazzling beacon, filling half the sky.

It looked a little like the earth, that huge world floating up there. There was one great bulging land mass that was very much like Africa, though it seemed too far to the south, and he couldn't find Europe where it ought to be, only a broad ocean occupying what might have been the place of the Mediterranean Sea. To the west Sean could make out something similar to the curve of North America's eastern seaboard, though the shape wasn't a perfect match with what he remembered, and the West Indies weren't there. Far down to the side was an enormous round hump of an island, vaguely in the position that South America once had had.

If that was earth, then, that loomed above him in the sky, it was an earth vastly transformed.

Earth? Up there in the sky? Then where was he? On the moon?

A garden of fragrant green and gold flowers rising on stalks of crystal – on the moon? Flowers on the moon? Sweet fresh air on the moon?

Nine and a half million years. Anything was possible.

He took a few steps. The pull of gravity seemed normal enough. It should feel almost like floating, he knew, to walk on the moon. Unless they had changed that, too. If they could give the moon an atmosphere and make gardens grow on it, they could give it earth-like gravitation also.

Should the earth look this close, though? He wasn't sure. He wished his astronomy was a little sharper. And his knowledge of geology, too. He knew that the continents drifted around, over the course of many millions of years, but could they have rearranged themselves so drastically in just nine and a half million years? Eric would know, of course. But Eric wasn't here.

The people of this era, Sean decided, can do anything they feel like doing. They can move the moon closer to the earth. They can move South America further from North America. Anything. Anything.

An age of miracles is what it must be.

He felt like an apeman suddenly swept millions of years forward into a world of telephones, television, computers and spaceships. Miracles. Miracles everywhere. And that was really what he was, he knew: a primitive creature, a prehistoric ape, a hairy, shambling, ancient man who needed to shave his face every day and who still carried an appendix around in his belly. How they must pity him, the unseen watchers who – he was entirely sure – were studying him now! Were they human at all? Did the human race still exist? Or had it died out long ago, and given way to some race of superbeings?

He reached down and let his fingers caress one of the lovely crystalline flowers.

It wriggled with pleasure like a cat being stroked, and began to sing, a slow, sinuous, sensuous melody. Immediately the others nearby started to preen and sway as if trying to get Sean's attention. *Touch me,* they were telling him. *Touch me, touch me, touch me! Make me sing!*

He was reminded of the garden of talking flowers that Alice had found in Looking-Glass Land: the vain and haughty Tiger-lily, and Rose, and Violet. How many times had he read that book, he and Eric! Eric had always liked Wonderland better; Sean had preferred the world beyond the looking-glass. And now here he was in Looking-Glass Land himself, where the flowers sang, and the blue earth hung in the sky instead of the moon.

'You like that, do you?' he asked the flowers.

And he stroked this one and that, reaching out towards them, going on down the garden row until hundreds of them were swaying and singing. The sweetness of their song was dream-like on the thick perfumed air. He had never heard anything so beautiful.

A great strange peace came over him. He felt a presence in his spirit. Something magical, something almost divine. Slowly he walked between the rows of flowers, savouring the mild night air, pausing often to stare up at the blue world that seemed so close overhead. It was an overwhelming privilege, being here in this place so many millions of years beyond his own time. He knew he would never see more of it than this garden, and that he would never understand any of it at all, but none of that mattered. He was here. He had been touched by something that was far beyond him as he was beyond the apes of the forests of humanity's dawn. Something magnificent. Something all-powerful. And yet, small as he was, splendid and mighty as it was, he felt a kinship with it. He was part of it; it was a part of him.

Then he thought of Eric, and the snarling, roaring, maddened giant ape that he was fated to meet head-on when it was his turn to arrive back there in that prehistoric jungle. And his mood of harmony and tranquility shattered.

At once the flowers began to sing a soothing song. He stared at them for a long while, not soothed, brooding about his brother. That ape looked really murderous. What if he kills Ricky, Sean thought? What happens to the experiment? What happens to the world? What happens to *me*? It was the big risk that they had all tried to make believe would not be a factor. But Sean had seen the look in that ape's eye.

If only I could warn him, he thought. But how? How?

To the flowers he said, 'I have to save my brother.'

They made a gentle humming sound.

He sat quietly, staring at a smooth, flat white rock, like a gleaming slab of marble, just in front of him in the garden.

An idea came to him.

'Forgive me,' he said. 'I've got to mess up this beautiful place a little. But it may be that the whole structure of the past and future depends on it.'

He took out his laser and turned it to high beam. And

began to write, carving a message on that flawless stone slab in ugly black charred letters.

RICKY — DANGER!!!

As concisely as he could, he told his brother when and where the ape was waiting for him in the time stream. And suggested in the strongest possible way that he had better have his anaesthetic dart gun primed and ready the moment he arrived.

'Do you think that'll do it?' he asked the flowers. 'Will he turn up here in this exact spot? Will he see the message? Will he be able to nail the ape in time?'

The flowers were singing again. Soothing, comforting sounds. Everything will be all right, they were saying. Everything will be fine.

I hope that's true, Sean thought, trying to relax.

Gradually the magic returned. This was too beautiful a place to be tangled up in fears and fretfulness for long.

He felt that celestial harmony again. He felt that peace, he felt that presence.

Then the flowers fell silent. He stared up at the shining earth with trembling wonder.

27

Eric $+ 5 \times 10^{13}$ minutes

Onwards—

—Onwards, unimaginably far—

He hovered in space, midway between somewhere and anywhere. There was a golden light all about him. Comets left dazzling trails in the void. Suns whirled and danced. He filled his hands with the stuff of space, warm and soft.

He felt like a god.

He *was* a god.

This was Time Ultimate. The power of the singularities that had propelled him through time reached its limit here. The world he knew lay ninety-five million years behind him. Here in this realm of light everything was utterly strange. He was drifting among the stars, far from earth. Earth? He could barely remember earth. He could barely remember himself, who he was, why and how he had come here. So far away now, so faint in his mind. All that noisy striving, all that energy, all that restless seeking.

The boiling cauldron that had been earth and its billions of people.

He knew that they had found whatever it was they had been seeking, those restless questing people, back in that time when earth still was. They had gained their answers long ago and they had become like gods. And earth was gone now, and they were gone with it, gone forth into the universe, into this shining kingdom.

They had touched the stars, and the stars had accepted them into their company. As they would accept him, pilgrim out of time that he was.

How can it be, he wondered, that I'm out here in space and still able to breathe?

And a quiet voice out of nowhere said, *While you are here, you will be as we are. And when you leave we will restore you to what you were.*

'Who are you?' he asked. 'Where are you? What are you?'

We are everyone. And we are everywhere. We are those for whom you prepared the way. And we protect you now and cherish you and welcome you among us.

'I see,' Eric said, and almost thought he did.

His long journey now seemed almost like a dream. Fragments of strange scenes floated through his mind: endlessly branching tunnels through which strange silent creatures marched, and a boy coming out of a small house on an earthquake-jumbled street, and vines flourishing in tropical heat, and squat, shaggy creatures gathered around a fire in a cave on a snowy hillside, and giant redwood trees rising like the columns of a cathedral, and an Englishman in riding clothes pointing to a hominid ape that had been extinct four million years, and a camel with the neck of a giraffe, and more, much more. A torrent of images. He had made a voyage beyond all belief; and it was not over yet, for soon the pendulum would be carrying him back down the eons, taking him to new wonders as he descended through time. But that was yet to come. He was here now, in the great stillness of the world beyond the world, dwelling among people who had touched the stars.

He, too, could touch the stars. He could reach out and embrace them and engulf them, and be engulfed by them. Here blazed a blue star, and here a white one, and here a giant red one in the forehead of the night, and he touched them all. And felt the throbbing weight of the billions of years of Creation upon him. And heard the soaring song of those who had gone forth before him into this realm of light. And drifted on the bosom of the firmament. And gave thanks. And joined in that great song.

28

Sean − 5×10^{13} minutes

There were dinosaurs all over the place. You walked around a bush and there was a dragon the size of a school bus eating its breakfast. You came over a hill and there was something that looked like an armoured tank taking its babies for a stroll. You looked up and a flotilla of pterodactyls went zooming by, flapping their long leathery wings.

It was a real zoo here. A Cretaceous zoo, fantastic monsters lumbering around everywhere. You had to look lively to keep from getting trampled on, of course. And there was always that itchy feeling between your shoulder blades that made you think a tyrannosaurus was coming up behind you, thinking about a snack.

The air was hot and dank. Gigantic ferns, big as palm trees, formed dark, humid forests. Dragonflies the size of hawks fluttered around, buzzing and droning.

'Ricky?' Sean said out loud. 'Ricky, you ought to see this! Man, you'd go *crazy!* This stuff is really wasted on me. But you, you old dinosaur freak—'

Well, Eric would be seeing all this soon enough, he knew. Unless something had happened to him during his zigzag voyage across the immensity of time. Sean didn't want to think about that possibility. Eric was all right. Eric *had* to be all right. And he'd be showing up here in a little while so that they could begin the homeward leg of their incredible journey.

This was Time Ultimate, the furthest swing of the pendulum. They had gone as far as they could go.

Right now Eric was somewhere out in the unthinkably remote future, ninety-five million years on the other side of Time Zero. And he, Sean, was here in the Cretaceous period, with a triceratops family grazing at the edge of the marsh and something that looked like a brontosaurus, but probably wasn't, rearing its snaky head high over the surface of the lake down there. But at any moment the force of the pendulum would be fully extended and he and Eric would start their downward swing, back towards Time Zero and the scientists waiting for them in the laboratory.

Sean had a pretty good idea of what it would be like. For an instant, time would seem to stand still. Then there would be a breathtaking plunge across the whole span of the displacement as he and Eric changed places. Eric would land here, among his beloved dinosaurs, and Sean would go swinging outwards into whatever unimaginable place the world of AD 95 million might be.

And then from there, it would be down the line for them. He would shoot into the world of nine and a half million years, and then to the one of 951,000 years in the future, and then to 95,000 years in the past, and so on all the way back, changing places with Eric at each level, one brother replacing the other without an instant of transition.

So Eric would visit the garden of miracles on the moon, Eric would have to cope with the charging giant ape, Eric would turn up at the Thanksgiving dinner that never was. Eric would have to deal with those bison-hunters back in Arizona. Eric would take his place in Quintu-Leela's arms and probably he too would be swept off into time too fast for it to matter. Eric would cheer at President Harding's inauguration parade. Eric would show up for the tail end of his own parade in Glendora.

And meanwhile . . . .

Sean stood leaning against a tree fern that was four times his own height, watching the parade of giant reptiles, and thinking of everything that had befallen him on his whirlwind trip through past and future. The world would never be the same, now that the gates of time stood wide open. And neither would he. His mind was full of such strange happenings as no other mortal being had ever experienced. None except Eric, at any rate.

Sean wondered what was in store for him in all those eras where Eric had already been.

Perils, thrills, bewilderments galore – no doubt of that. And perhaps some burst of sudden ecstasy to match or even surpass that mystical moment among the singing flowers that glowed by the light of the full earth in the sky.

He'd know, soon enough. He could feel the force tugging at him now, starting to take him onwards.

He smiled. He slapped the tree fern fondly, as if saying goodbye to an old friend, and went strolling down towards the lake. His boots make sucking noises. It was all wet, spongy swampland here. The dinosaurs all around him snorted and mooed and grunted as they went about their business.

They didn't know what he was, and they didn't care. They were lords of the world and they could look forward to millions of years more of snorting and mooing and grunting in this warm, leafy kingdom of theirs. Eric was going to have the time of his life when he got here. How he would hate it, when the force pulled him away. As it was pulling Sean, now.

The pull was getting stronger.

So long, triceratops. So long, pterodactyls. So long, whatever-you-are with the spikes on your back. I'm moving along. But Eric's coming to take my place. He's okay, Ricky is. You and he will get along pretty well.

Going away, now. Moving up and out. Heading for the downswing, starting the journey back, everything running in reverse.

Until at last it all came winding down to the starting point, and he and Eric would step off the shunt platform in the very moment of their departures. Or so it would seem to everyone else. But the strangeness wouldn't end there. Five minutes later, $Sean_2$ would materialize in that lab, and $Eric_2$ also. And again, eight hours after that. And again in three days. And again and again and again, throughout all the rest of their lives and far beyond. He and Ricky were destined to appear like comets, he knew, showing up at fixed intervals across the ninety-five million years that followed Time Zero. While at the same time they would be trying to live their ordinary lives through to their normal spans, doing whatever it was that they were destined to do until the time came to grow old and die. With ninety-five million years of life still waiting for them.

That was going to be really strange. To know in 2025 that yourself of nine and a half years earlier was going to show up out of time. And then ninety-five years later to have it happen again, if they were lucky enough to live to that kind of an age – and probably many people would, by then.

Going away now. Time to be starting for home, by way of the year AD 95 million.

Sean saw the dinosaurs fade and grow misty.

Time seemed to stand still for a billion billion years. The pendulum had reached the balance point.

And he saw Ricky.

His twin brother hovered in the air just in front of him, shimmering like a vision. Sean realized that he was probably shimmering just the same way. This was the moment of turnaround, when all the forces were equalling out, and it was like no other moment in the trip.

'Ricky?' he said. 'Ricky, can you hear me?'

Sean saw his brother's lips move. He was saying something, asking something. But he was unable to hear Ricky's voice. They were still cut off from each other by the barrier of time. And yet not really cut off, for he could look straight into his brother's eyes. He knew now that Ricky had come through everything okay. And that they were going to make it back to the starting point at Time Zero, too.

And he saw the look of wonder shining in Ricky's eyes.

He has seen miracles, Sean thought. Different miracles from the ones I've seen, but miracles all the same. The ones that I'm heading for now.

'Ricky?' Sean said again. 'Hey, Ricky. Look! Here come your dinosaurs, man! Here come your dinosaurs at last!'

He waved and smiled. And Eric smiled and waved back at him.

'See you back at Time Zero!' Sean called. 'And watch out for that oversized monkey!' But he knew that the ape wasn't going to be a problem. Ricky would see the message in the garden on the moon. Ricky would be quick on the draw with the anaesthetic darts. His shimmering presence here left Sean with no doubts that the experiment was going to go successfully right to the end.

Eric was vanishing now. Growing faint, growing insubstantial.

No, Sean thought. I'm the one who's vanishing. He's coming, I'm going. So long, dinosaurs! Here I go!

The moment at the balance point was over. The pendulum was moving again. Carrying him off into the mists of time to come.

Sean didn't want the voyage ever to end, not really. But at the same time he knew that he did. So that he could get back to Time Zero, and Eric. To tell him about everything he had seen. And to hear about what had happened to him. He needed to share every detail of the voyage, and he knew that Ricky did, too. No one else could possibly understand.

They were going to have plenty to tell each other, Sean knew. Enough to last them for the rest of their lives.